PARANORMAL COZY MYSTERY

Tracks & Flashbacks

TRIXIE SILVERTALE

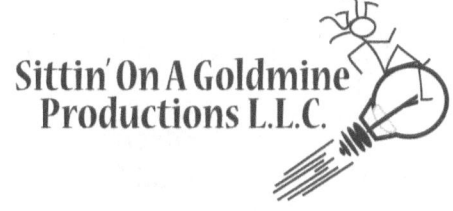

Sittin' On A Goldmine
Productions L.L.C.

Sittin' On A Goldmine Productions, L.L.C.

pr@sittinonagoldmine.co

www.sittinonagoldmine.co

ISBN: 978-1-952739-09-5

Cover Design © Sittin' On A Goldmine Productions, L.L.C.

Trixie Silvertale
Tracks and Flashbacks: Paranormal Cozy Mystery : a novel / by Trixie Silvertale — 1st ed.

[1. Paranormal Cozy Mystery — Fiction. 2. Cozy Mystery — Fiction. 3. Amateur Sleuths — Fiction. 4. Female Sleuth — Fiction. 5. Wit and Humor — Fiction.] 1. Title.

CHAPTER 1

THERE'S A MOMENT in every relationship when you either cut and run, or you push your chips to the middle of the table and say, "All in."

Last night felt like that moment, but . . .

As liquid streaks of grey cascade across the sky and quench the stars, I stare out the 6 x 6 windows of my swanky apartment and rub the residue of dreams from my eyes. I don't remember falling asleep, and I don't remember Erick leaving, but it was sweet of him to put a blanket over me before he did.

A rustling on the richly carpeted floor draws my attention. I lazily roll over, and my breath catches in my throat.

There, on my floor, in my apartment—is a man!

Warmth and happiness swirl in my belly. He's possibly the most thoughtful man in the entire world. Sheriff Erick Harper is sound asleep, with one arm folded under his tousled blond hair. His fitted button-down shirt is wrinkled and bunched up in a way that exposes a sliver of his perfect abs above the edge of his hand-sanded blue jeans.

It takes every drop of my imaginary self-control to stay firmly planted on the over-stuffed settee, while each fiber of my being is begging to be the "little spoon."

He yawns, stretches adorably, and rolls onto his back. But before I can take the inevitable day-dreams of a film-school dropout any further, my en-titled feline slinks across the floor and steals my place.

The large tan caracal known as Pyewacket gently climbs onto Erick's broad chest and circles into a cozy pile.

Sheriff Too-Hot-To-Handle stirs, and his first instinct is to look toward the couch.

Busted! I blush and duck my snow-white haystack of hair under the blanket.

He chuckles.

Letting one of my curious grey eyes peek out, my insides go all gooey as I watch him interact with my four-legged master.

Erick reaches a tentative hand toward Pyewacket's head. "Hey, guy, are we friends now?" His long, sexy fingers scratch between Pye's ears.

The normally fiendish feline presses his broad skull into the proffered people tentacles and, despite his disdain for humanity at large, purrs loudly.

It's official, even my cantankerous cat is team Erick! I throw back my blanket and prepare to scold the furry traitor—

A sudden streak of ghostly mist above my head stops me cold.

"I stayed away as long as I could, dear. I didn't interrupt your—"

I clench my teeth together with all my might, thankful that I'm the only one who can see and hear this ghost-rusion! Taking a deep breath, I think-scream a telepathic warning to my otherworldly intruder. *Grams! Get out of here immediately. The last thing I need is for Erick to experience ghost-chills and start asking questions! Get back to the museum side of things and keep working on your memoirs. I'll fill you in on the details after breakfast.*

The ghost of my "not as dead as everyone thinks" grandmother flickers in and out like a freeze-frame on an old VHS tape. Her burgundy silk-and-tulle designer gown shimmers as she places a bejeweled fist on her ample hip. "Well, I hope everyone used protection."

And as she phase-shifts out of the apartment, I

think one last warning in her wake: *None of your business!*

But between you and me, it wasn't *that* kind of sleepover.

"Am I gonna need to send someone in there after you?" Erick's sly grin is slipping toward concern.

I'm too sleepy to feign innocence, so I use the most convenient tool at my disposal. "Were you talking to me? I thought you were talking to Pye."

He shakes his head. "I was starting to think that maybe you sleep with your eyes open. Normally when I mention food, especially food at Myrtle's Diner, you're the first person to vote yes."

My hand shoots into the air. "I vote yes." The rest of my body lacks my arm's conviction. I sluggishly get to my feet. "Hey, why did you sleep on the floor? I mean, the bed was empty."

He shrugs and looks at the floor. "You were on the couch— I didn't want— It didn't feel right. The floor was fine. Trust me, on my second tour in Afghanistan, I slept on top of a row of fifty-gallon fuel drums in the belly of a C-47. Compared to that, this carpet was heaven."

Wriggling my bare toes in the lush wall-to-wall, I chuckle. "It is pretty great carpet. Give me a minute to change and we'll be good to go."

Erick cautiously transfers Pyewacket to the

well-cushioned floor, sits up, and runs a hand through his long, loose blond bangs. "No way, Moon. If I've gotta do the walk of shame, I'm not walking alone."

Giggling, I straighten my dress and attempt an uncoordinated curtsy. "As you wish." I plunk back down on the settee, retrieve my strappy sandals, and strap in. "I can barely walk in these things awake and sober. So, I'm definitely gonna require assistance, half-asleep with a Chianti hangover."

He's instantly by my side. "Too much wine? Do you need aspirin or a glass of water?"

This man cannot be real. He's already got me wrapped around his little finger. What more does he want?

As if in answer to my unspoken thought, he slips an arm around my waist and leans close. "Can you ignore my morning breath?"

My tummy flip-flops and my skin tingles. I lean toward him and let my eyelids flutter. "I will if you will."

He closes the distance and his soft, full lips taste of possibilities and promises, while the stubble on his chin brings me back to reality. A flush spreads over his cheeks as he leans away and clears his throat. "Well, we better get to breakfast. I'm sure we could both use some coffee."

Inside my head, I do a little shoulder shimmy and whisper to myself, "Still got it."

Following him toward the hidden exit, I push the plaster medallion of twisting ivy, and the secret bookcase door slides open.

Erick exhales, once again impressed, despite having seen it before. He offers me his elbow and steadies me as I navigate between the perfectly aligned rows of oak desks in the Rare Books Loft. I firmly grip the wrought-iron railing and spiral my way down the narrow staircase to the first floor of my bookshop.

When we emerge into the summer sun on Main Street, I shiver as a colder than expected blast of wind hurls itself up from the great lake tucked in the harbor behind my store.

He pulls me close and shares his bodily warmth as we head toward the diner.

Myrtle's Diner is a Pin Cherry Harbor staple. My grandmother, Myrtle Isadora, and her first husband, Odell, started the diner decades ago. He even received a commendation from the Pin Cherry Harbor Historical Society earlier this year.

All eyes turn as Erick holds the door open for me. I attempt to strut casually across the black-and-white linoleum, and, as quickly as possible, slide into a booth without drawing any additional attention.

Of course, drawing attention in a small town is as easy as breathing. In fact, lack of air is unlikely to stop gossip.

Erick scoots onto the red-vinyl bench seat opposite me, and my favorite waitress, Tally, places two coffees on the table before either of us can speak.

She nods her head, and the tightly wound, flame-red bun atop her head bobs in unison. "That gonna be enough creamer, honey?"

Glancing at the melamine bowl filled with individual creamers, I smile. "That should be enough for the first two cups. I'll let you know how it's looking if we have to go for cup number three."

Her eyes track from me to the sheriff and back. She winks and returns to the kitchen.

After a long sip of coffee, I find the strength to glance toward the galley.

My surrogate grandpa is grinning down at the grill like an idiot, and pretending he didn't see me walk in. But I can already smell my breakfast cooking, and I'm more than familiar with his reputation for knowing exactly what his regular clients need before they do.

Erick gazes across the table at me, and one corner of his mouth lifts in a smirk that says, "We have a secret, and I like it."

Before I can provide an adequate response, the all-too-familiar sound of polyester squeaking against vinyl pricks the hairs on the back of my neck. Sure enough, a few seconds later, the pudgy, self-important shape of Deputy Paulsen darkens the end of our table. "Little early for a fancy dress, Moon." Her gaze glides over my outfit with disdain.

Despite my desire to keep my relationship with Erick as discreet as possible, this woman always gets under my skin. "Or perhaps it's actually a bit late." I arch one eyebrow in what I hope indicates that I am ending a date rather than starting one.

Based on the widening of her eyes and the increase in her heart rate, picked up by my extrasensory perceptions, I'd say she received the message.

"See ya at the station, Sheriff." Her hand slips to its usual resting place on the handle of her gun and she waddles out of the diner.

Erick walks his fingers across the table and turns up his palm. But before I can slip my hand into his, Odell arrives with two steaming plates of deliciousness.

He sets a large stack of blueberry pancakes and sausage in front of Erick, while I receive my usual scrambled eggs, chorizo, golden-delicious home fries, and a bottle of Tabasco. Glancing back and forth between the occupants of his booth, he asks, "Anything I need to know?"

There's no judgment in his query, but the authority in his prior-military voice definitely connects with the former soldier in Erick.

"No, sir."

Odell and I have always had a straightforward relationship, so I choose to give him a little more information. "Actually, it looks like I'll be heading back to Arizona for a week or two. I'm sure Twiggy can take care of Pyewacket, but I wouldn't mind if you'd drive past the bookshop on your way home at night, just to make sure everything's all right."

He nods an affirmative, raps his knuckles twice on the silver-flecked white Formica table, and returns to the kitchen.

Erick exhales a nervous breath and picks up his knife and fork.

I lean back and smile. "So, I've been meaning to ask you, does Odell outrank you?"

His face scrunches up in confusion, before a humble slouch tips his shoulders forward. "Someday you're going to have to tell me how it is you have such accurate *hunches*. Odell managed to make his way up to staff sergeant. I had a little more trouble with authority during my tours in Afghanistan. I made sergeant before I got out, but only by the skin of my teeth. So, technically, yeah . . . He outranks me."

A self-satisfied smile drifts across my face before I dive into my yummy breakfast. There's nothing like a pile of home fries and a good cup of coffee to kick out the last vestiges of a hangover. "I better head back to the bookstore and see about travel arrangements. Are you sure you want to go?"

He walks his fingers back across the table, and this time we successfully clasp hands without interruption. "Moon, after the kind of trouble you've gotten yourself into since you came to Pin Cherry Harbor, there is literally no way I'm not going to Arizona."

"Rude."

He shrugs his shoulders. "But accurate."

I have to laugh at my own misfortune. "You're not wrong. I guess stumbling upon corpses, following my hunches, and solving crimes has gotten me into more than my share of trouble. It would be nice to have someone with me."

"Any chance you'll show me around your old haunts in Sedona before we dive into the case?"

"You're kidding, right?"

He laughs openly. "It was worth a shot."

"Not on your life, Sheriff. When, not if, we solve this case, we'll celebrate properly in Sedona."

"10-4."

"I think you meant to say, 'Copy that.'"

He laughs and his eyes follow me longingly as I slide out of the booth.

My skin tingles anew, and I'm so distracted I almost forget to bus my dishes. As I leave the diner, I wave to Tally and Odell, and he gives me a spatula salute through the red-Formica-trimmed orders-up window.

CHAPTER 2

It's not until I walk back to the Bell, Book & Candle Bookshop and reach for the handle of my delicately carved wooden door that it comes to my attention that I left without my keys. I was so distracted by Erick's presence and the possibility of Grams reappearing at any moment . . . I didn't really think things through.

I wander down First Street toward the alley that passes between my bookshop/printing museum and my father's building, which houses the Duncan Restorative Justice Foundation. Fortunately for me, he's traveling on business. So the good news is, I won't have to tell him face-to-face about my trip to Arizona.

I ring the bell next to the alleyway door and the

familiar BING BONG BING resounds inside the bookshop.

My volunteer employee and my grandmother's best friend in life, Twiggy, isn't in yet, so I hope Grams responds to the bell and has enough ghost juice to help a girl out.

"Mitzy, is that you?"

"Hooray! Grams, I left without my keys. Do you think you have enough in the tank to physically manipulate the door handle?"

A light chuckle passes through the door. "As you are so fond of saying, on one condition."

My shoulders slouch. "Which is?"

She clears her throat dramatically on the other side of the door. "On the condition that you tell me exactly what happened last night, and don't sugar-coat it."

I throw my hands up in the air. "You win. Once again, I have no private life. Apparently I exist solely for your amusement, and Twiggy's entertainment."

I swear there's a paranormal snicker.

In case I forgot to mention, Twiggy doesn't accept any money in exchange for her work at the bookshop. It seems that the amusement she gains from being privy to my physical and relationship-based clumsiness is all the payment she needs.

The lock turns and the handle jiggles. "You'll have to pull it, sweetie. That's all I've got left. I was working on the second draft of my memoirs all night."

Grasping the handle, I pull open the heavy metal door and slip into my shop. Pyewacket bursts from the shadows and figure-eights through my legs.

"Poor little fur baby."

He allows me to scratch his head and rub one of his black-tufted ears.

"I'm sorry I went to breakfast without pouring your Fruity Puffs. Seems like I was more distracted than I realized."

Stepping into the back room, I fill his bowl with an award-winning-sized portion of sugary children's cereal. "You are the most spoiled animal in all of Christendom. However, you were very sweet to Erick this morning, and it didn't go unnoticed."

"Ree-ow." Soft but condescending.

Shaking my head at the impudence of the four-legged demon spawn, I hoof it upstairs. "All right, Grams, buckle up. It's going to be a bumpy ride."

She pantomimes buckling a seatbelt around her gown.

"On the short drive over to Angelo and Vinci's, I felt some weird waves of emotion coming from Erick. My senses picked up that he mostly felt filled with anticipation, but every now and then there was a strange stabbing pain."

"I thought you promised to use your powers for good, dear. Sounds like you were snooping around his insides." Grams arches a perfectly drawn brow.

"I wasn't doing it on purpose. I mean, I didn't go digging for it. It was more like that catcher's mitt 'let the messages come to you' thing that Silas taught me."

"Whatever you need to tell yourself." She crosses her translucent arms.

"Moving on." I glare at her meaningfully. "When we arrived, he asked me to wait in the car so he could open my door—"

"Such a gentleman!" She accompanies her exclamation with a dramatic clutching of her pearls.

"Grams! I'll never finish this story if you keep interrupting."

"Please continue, dear."

"He wore a super cute pair of blue hand-sanded jeans and this button-down shirt that fit him so perfectly. Plus, he let his hair hang a little looser—no pomade. You know how much I like it when his bangs are casual." I look to Grams for confirmation.

She pantomimes a key locking her lips and tucks the invisible key in her bosom.

"Oh brother." Rolling my eyes for emphasis, I continue my tale.

"He took my hand, pulled me up quickly and planted a little kiss on my cheek." I attempt to leave out the part about how his citrus-woodsy smell made me a little weak in the knees.

However, my thought-dropping Ghost-ma grins and puts a hand over her mouth in mock surprise.

I breeze through the particulars of the restaurant décor and menu. "But I couldn't ignore the tense vibe coming from him. I kinda started to worry that he was going to break up with me."

"He wouldn't dare!" Ghost wrath spills from Isadora's eyes and I have to take a step back.

"The server kept showing up at the worst times and totally jacking our flow. And it took forever to get my glass of wine."

A judgmental glare from the spirit of the recovering alcoholic burns down from on high.

Flicking her issues away, I exhale. "As always, Grams, I respect your struggle, but I'm not an alcoholic and I'm allowed to enjoy a glass of wine."

She scoffs and gestures to the takeout containers and the two empty Chianti bottles on the coffee table.

"Point taken." Flopping onto the four-poster bed, I tuck two perfect pillows behind my head and sink into the glorious sheets. "After we got rid of the server, he announced that he had a present for me, but thought he should wait until after dinner. I quickly informed him that there was pretty much no way I could eat anything until I got the rest of the story."

She wiggles the curvy hips that I clearly inherited.

"While he ate a couple breadsticks, I proposed a halfhearted toast. I said something like, 'Ready when you are, Sheriff.' Then he laid a manila envelope on the table and everything felt as though it switched into slow motion. I couldn't figure out if it was going to be some terrible coroner's report or something fantastic, like when Silas delivered the envelope that revealed how the grandmother I'd never met had left me a fortune and an amazing bookshop."

Ghost-ma blows me a kiss and nods her acceptance of my gratitude.

"He kept saying how he honestly meant it as a gift, which made me feel worse." I take a moment to swallow. "When I upended the envelope, this was the first thing that fell out." I reach toward my chest and reverently touch the sterling-silver dream-catcher necklace with its three silver feathers and the tiny amethyst crystal at its center.

Ethereal hands extend toward the pendant and I feel Grams' love.

"It was my mother's. I couldn't imagine how he got it."

She smiles, and I can see the tears pushing at

the corners of her eyes.

"I started to cry, of course. The server probably thought I was getting dumped. But actually this amazing guy went totally out of his way to try and make sure I had something of my mom's. He said he knew I was eleven when she passed away, and since I went into the foster system, he thought maybe no one had ever collected her personal effects. He called in a favor from the Maricopa County Sheriffs —for me."

Now we're both crying, and my unrealized dreams of getting her an afterlife hankie resurface.

Catching my breath and wiping my cheeks, I continue, "I assumed the necklace was the good part, but I knew there had to be something bad in the envelope because he was acting so bajiggity."

"Forgive the interruption, dear. But I don't remember—"

"Oh, right. Bajiggity means agitated or anxious, but in an extra weird way."

She nods.

"I told him I didn't want to make a scene in the restaurant and he immediately apologized for taking me to a public place. He said he'd ask them to package everything up to-go and we'd look through the rest of it in my apartment."

"He really is the sweetest man."

"My ring was buzzing with messages, but I

couldn't handle it. When Erick came back, he helped me put on the necklace and I felt closer to my mom right away."

Grams dabs at her eyes with the back of her translucent hand.

"You obviously know what happened when we got back, because you attacked me as soon as we walked through the door, and almost made me slip up in front of Erick."

Grams can't stand my misinterpretation. "My version is that I was concerned, but as soon as you asked me to leave I did. And, let the record show that I did not pop in once during your date. However, I was a little shocked to find Sheriff Harper still in your apartment this morning."

"It's not what you think. The restaurant actually delivered the food and they brought two bottles of wine instead of one. Once I opened that envelope and discovered that the commuter train that hit my mom's car was a cover up, I didn't want to be alone."

"So you slept with Erick to forget about your mother's murder?"

"Rude! And no. For the eleven millionth time, we did not sleep together. I mean, we both slept in this apartment, but I slept on the settee and he slept on the floor like a perfect gentleman."

Grams tilts her head in a way that neither rejects nor accepts my claim.

"I was so overwhelmed to have this necklace . . . I don't know if I'll ever be able to express to him how much it means to me." Tears trickle down my cheeks. "The envelope contained a photo of my mom, her old driver's license, some personal stuff, a copy of the police report, and the coroner's report."

"How did she die?" Grams sighs and shakes her head.

"According to the coroner's report, the cause of death was undetermined. Erick thinks the crash was an attempt to cover up any evidence that would point to the murder. Basically, she was working as a confidential informant for the Phoenix Metro Police Department, and somehow her cover was blown and somebody killed her to suppress whatever evidence she had."

"Who murdered her, dear?"

"Erick said it's unsolved." I sigh and take a ragged breath. "That's why we're going to Arizona. I'm going to thaw out this cold case and make sure my mom's killer gets locked up for good."

"Good for you." Grams nods furiously. "The very thought of some no-good low-life taking a single mother from her child! You dish up some justice, Mitzy." She hesitates. "You did say 'we' didn't you?"

I swipe at the tears on my cheeks. "As soon as I

announced that I was going to crack the case, Erick said that he had a lot of vacation days saved up that he'd never taken."

"Oh, that dear boy." She fans herself and then clutches one of her many strands of pearls.

"Right? He said somebody has to keep the new Sundance Kid out of the hoosegow." I chuckle, and Grams smiles broadly. "So, that opened the floodgates and I cried for what seemed like forever. Once I got that out of my system, we started pouring wine and talking. The hours disappeared, the wine disappeared, and I woke up on the settee with a blanket covering me."

Grams swirls closer and uses the last sparks of her energy to rub my back compassionately.

A moment later she flickers out of existence.

"Grams? Grams! Are you still here? Please tell me this isn't like the time I lost you! I can't handle that right now."

A faint voice drifts through the ether. "I'm here, dear. I'm just so weak."

A shaky exhale escapes and my heart stops its uncontrollable thudding. "That's a load off. Go recharge or whatever it is you need to do. I have to take care of the travel arrangements, but I'll leave the packing until you're feeling up to it."

A warm sparkle circles near my left cheek and vanishes with a snap.

CHAPTER 3

SITTING ALONE IN MY APARTMENT, I feel that old familiar orphan ache. I may have inherited a fortune, and some amazing real estate, but the one thing that truly matters to me is the family I discovered in Pin Cherry Harbor. I can't imagine what I would do if I truly lost Ghost-ma.

Stepping out of my apartment, I let my toes curl into the lovely Persian carpets in the Rare Books Loft. I slip *Saducismus Triumphatus* from the shelf, carefully lay it on one of the oak reading tables, and pull the brass chain dangling beneath the green-glass shade. Crisp light brightens the pages. I lean back in the chair and take a deep breath.

This place holds so much more than books. The scent of age, mystery, and endless possibilities hangs heavy in the air. The view calls to me. I walk toward the railing and gaze across the rows and rows of bookcases on the first floor. As the light filters through the 6 x 6 slumped-glass windows at the front and bounces dreamily off the tin-plated ceiling, it illuminates the dust moats floating through the air.

Being a massive fangirl of all things film and television, it's easy for me to imagine each speck as a traveler from another dimension, floating through the bookshop in search of a tome that will portal them to their home world.

Am I really going back to Arizona? That medical examiner's report is the story, the portal, that's pulling me into a universe of memories I'd just as soon forget.

Pyewacket slinks across the mezzanine and drops a business card at my feet.

"I haven't even told you about my case, Pye. You can't possibly know who murdered my mother already." I bend and pick up the business card. "However, it sure would save me a lot of time if you did."

"RE-OW!" Game on!

Chuckling, I glance at the business card. It touts Howie Fairlane as the Great White North's only IT Specialist.

"I'm sure you're trying to help, buddy, but you know as well as I do that Pin Cherry Harbor doesn't *do* technology. The fact that we have an ancient computer in the back room that only Twiggy knows how to operate is more of an anomaly than a standard. I'm pretty sure I don't need an information technology expert."

I walk toward the brass wastepaper bin at the top of the stairs and receive a firm warning THWACK to my left calf. And to be clear, I know it's a warning, because the needle-like claws remain retracted.

Spinning toward the fiend, I demand more information. "All right. I'll call Howie Fairlane. But before I do, it would be stellar if you'd explain to me what exactly I'm going to ask this man."

Pyewacket tilts his head in a way that makes me feel like the inferior species and struts over to the bookcase that serves as the secret entrance to my apartment. He looks back over his shoulder, irritated that I am so slow on the uptake.

I pull down the candle sconce and the bookcase slides open.

My four-legged guide struts into the apartment, leaps up onto the coffee table, and swats my mobile phone onto the floor with one paw.

Crouching to retrieve the phone, I'm eye to eye with my reluctant teacher. "So it has something to do with my phone? But my phone works perfectly. Like I said, I don't need an IT—"

Before I can finish my sentence Pyewacket lays his head on the phone and looks up at me with pleading golden eyes.

"What are you saying? You want your own phone?" I gasp and shake my head. "I could barely be convinced to give a child his or her own phone! How in the world do you expect me to justify giving a phone to a cat! You've lost it this time. You've well and truly lost it, son."

I toss my phone on the settee, but before I can stand, Pyewacket's claws dart out and grip the dreamcatcher necklace around my neck.

For a psychic, I can be pretty stupid. Images of Arizona montage through the magicked mood ring on my left hand as a chill encircles my ring finger.

"I'm sorry to be such a slow learner. You truly are a genius. I wish I could bring you to Arizona, but you'll have to stay here and take care of Grams. You know she's not going to handle my absence very well."

"Reow." Can confirm.

"But I get it." I pick up the business card and fan it between us. "I'll call Howie and see if he can set up some kind of telecommunication device that's simple enough to be operated by a very smart kitty. Is that what you were trying to tell me, Mr. Cuddlekins?"

"Re-ow." Thank you.

"First, I have to get Silas over here to prepare me for my trip."

After a brief call to my alchemist/attorney, he agrees to come to the bookshop for consultation. However, he doesn't miss the opportunity to admonish me for assuming alchemy is some website where I simply place things in my cart and check out at will.

By the time I'm out of the shower and into my standard skinny jeans topped by a T-shirt that reads "Never trust atoms, they make up everything," the patient, but put upon, voice of my mentor crackles from the intercom.

"Good day, Mizithra. Shall I come up?"

Crossing the room, I depress the mother-of-pearl button on the left and reply, "Yes, please." See how polite I can be, when I remember?

The bookcase door swooshes open, and Silas gestures to the thick tome lying open on one of the tables. "Some light reading?"

I chuckle. "Maybe. I was waxing nostalgic. I don't know. Either way, I got distracted by some dust motes and forgot to put it away."

Silas harrumphs into his bushy grey mustache. "The study of alchemy is no place for distraction. Lack of attention, in combination with your rare gifts, could have disastrous side effects."

My shoulders slump. "Sorry."

"It is not necessary for you to apologize. It would be far better for you to take corrective action."

"Copy that." I gesture for him to come in and have a seat in the scalloped-back chair.

I take the settee and bring him up to speed on the gift from Erick, and the complications that spilled out of the envelope that arrived from Arizona.

As usual, Silas makes no direct reply. Instead he follows his own agenda. "What is your mother's name?"

Tilting my head and scrunching up my face, I shrug and point to the papers. "It's in the report."

Silas does not look at the papers on the coffee table. Instead, his eyes lock on to me like a laser targeting system. "What is your mother's name?"

The hairs on the back of my neck stand on end and my mood ring burns mercilessly on my left hand, but I can't look away. "I don't want to say."

"You must. We must speak the names of the dead, lest they be forgotten. Lest her life has been in vain." His gaze softens and his voice is barely a whisper. "What is your mother's name?"

Tears well up in my eyes and a knot tightens in my stomach. Pressure in my chest feels as though it will squeeze all the air out of my lungs.

Silas patiently waits.

"Coraline Moon." I sniffle and swipe at the tears tumbling down my cheeks. "Mostly everyone called her Cora."

"Coraline Moon must have been fiercely independent, and she clearly loved you deeply. I am pleased you will convey the person or persons who took her life to justice. However, this cannot be a journey of vengeance. It must be an exploration, and, ultimately, a restoration of your mother's place in your heart."

My eyes widen and the pain in my chest seems unbearable. "What do you mean? My mom's always been in my heart."

"It is natural that you felt resentment at being abandoned in your youth. You no longer have a child's understanding of the world. Your mother's love was not diminished by her untimely demise. Follow her tracks, uncover her secrets, and in the end you will find what was taken from you so long ago."

Silent tears sluice down my cheeks, and Pyewacket leaps into my lap, pushing his head against me, in an attempt to drive away the pain. I scratch my fingers into the coarse fur on his back and struggle to catch my breath. "Thank you, Silas."

"How may I help you prepare for this endeavor?"

Wiping away the remainder of salty drops on

my cheeks, I take a deep breath, shake my arms and shoulders, and sigh. "Right. I don't remember if I mentioned that Erick offered to come with me?"

Silas nods. "That is most fortunate."

"It's pretty fortunate. But I'm kind of concerned about being alone with him for so long. What if I mess up and say something about my visions, or talk about Grams in the present tense, or blurt out something about alchemy?"

"I have always counseled truth as the best defense."

I shake my head. "I'm not you. I'm not at that place in my relationship with Erick. I'm not okay with it. All right?"

"Wherefore, it is your decision. How may I assist?"

"Well, what if I slip up? Is there some spell, I mean, alchemical transmutation that can kind of erase my mistake?"

Silas leans back in the over-stuffed chair, steeples his fingers, and bounces his jowly chin on the pointers. "Transmutations involving memory can be dangerous."

"But you taught me the truth symbols. I totally learned to use those and never hurt anyone. Can't you teach me something like that?"

He continues to bounce his chin and I feel a

lesson brewing. "What is your desired outcome for your return to the desert?"

"I want to figure out who killed my mom." My fists clench. "I want to make sure they pay."

The slow and methodical bouncing continues. "And what is Sheriff Harper's role in this journey?"

"He said he wanted to keep me safe. He says I have a habit of getting myself into trouble and he didn't want me to travel alone."

"Indeed."

It would seem that more than acknowledging Erick's role, Silas is siding with him regarding my ability to get into trouble. "Is there something you can teach me?"

His hands slowly move to his lap and he harrumphs before responding. "There are many things I may teach you, Mizithra. Lifetimes of things. However, today's time is short and your need is questionable. I shall impart the wisdom of the reversal runes if you swear to me that you will only employ their effect in the most dire of circumstances."

Careful to suppress my eagerness, I steady my breathing and lace my fingers together to keep my hands from shaking. "I swear."

CHAPTER 4

SILAS LEADS the way into the Rare Books Loft and procures a small book, sheathed in blood-red leather, from the bottom shelf of one of the bookcases. He lays the volume on an oak reading table and pulls the chain dangling below the green-glass lampshade. A bright light illuminates the pages, and the scent of secrets wafts toward me as he strokes the gilt edging and carefully leafs through the folios. Eventually, he stops and motions for me to join him beside the table. "The symbols here have many meanings. Connecting them in the precise order, which I will demonstrate, is the key to loosening the memory from its resting place. The power of the runes flows through you and takes its form from you. It cannot be undone." He leans back in the wooden chair and looks at me. "If you create the symbols incorrectly or execute them in the improper order you will certainly erase more than you intend—or perchance plant something false."

The film student in me hears a warning drum swell; sadly there's no such soundtrack in my real life. "Understood."

Silas tips his head and concern swirls in his milky-blue eyes. "I hope you truly do understand. This type of alchemy must be wielded judiciously."

He shows me the first symbol.

I retrace it with my finger. "Easy enough. What's next?"

His spine straightens in that alchemical-wizardy way that I always find unsettling.

Before he can scold me, I recite the warning he issued during my previous lesson, months ago. "I know these are not a child's doodles. I understand that symbols have power. I accept that this power must be accessed through focused intentionality. I promise not to be flippant." For some reason I'm holding my right hand up as though I'm being sworn into office.

He nods his solemn approval of my recitation. "You are correct. The things I teach you are not party tricks; they may have already saved your life— on more than one occasion." He turns away to hide his emotion from me.

I politely make no comment.

Silas demonstrates the three remaining symbols.

I repeat each of his motions with careful reverence.

"Now we must test your skill."

For some reason my heart races and my courage wavers. "I've got it. But I think I should practice more, you know?"

"When does your flight leave?"

"In the morning—"

"Tell me something you do not want me to remember." Silas gazes at me expectantly.

"Like how I stole some of Pyewacket's cereal?"

A hiss from the shadows confirms we are not alone, and I'm on notice.

"Not a trivial speck of waste. Reveal to me something you have never told another living soul. This information must matter to you, and the need to take the information back from me must burn deep within your heart."

I swallow audibly. The first thing that pops into my head scares me half to death and I search desperately through my grey matter for something less vital.

"No. You must use the thing you fear. If there is no true risk there can be no concrete reward." He nods, encouraging me to tell my secret.

A self-conscious heat prickles across my face. "I'm madly in love with Erick Harper."

Silas offers no opinion on the matter. He extends his right hand. "You must trace the symbols on the flesh of your target. Please begin."

I reach a shaky hand toward his palm.

"Perhaps a deep, steadying breath is in order." He continues to wait patiently.

Closing my eyes, I draw the breath. Without opening them, I place my finger in his palm and begin, tracing each symbol with serene intention. After the first three are complete a wave of self-doubt washes over me and I hesitate.

"You must not stop." His tone is even, but my psychic senses feel an unease beneath the surface.

Exhaling, I complete the final symbol and step back.

Silas smiles perfunctorily. "Are you ready for a test?"

My eyes widen. It can't possibly have worked that fast. "Do you remember what I told you?"

"Certainly. You admitted to pilfering Pyewacket's cereal."

"And that's all?"

"Indeed?"

"You don't remember the other thing? The super-secret thing?"

His expression transforms before my eyes. "It

would appear you are a more skilled student than I imagined."

"I don't know. I hesitated between the third and fourth symbols. I started to lose my nerve." I shrug.

"My mind and I are appreciative of your tenacity." His eyes warm with pride, but instantly chill. "You must remember that this transmutation is akin to playing God. It is not to be taken lightly and never to be used glibly."

All I can do is nod. My voice is locked inside my constricted throat. Now that I know the symbols, I'm not sure if I want the responsibility.

"You may require some additional items for your travels. May we return to the apartment?"

Once again, I nod.

Back inside, Silas approaches the large rectangular piece of decorative trim below one of the built-in bookcases. I recently learned that a hidden drawer pops out when you press on the center of this panel.

He pokes around the contents and extracts a pendulum, a small amber vial, and a stone with a hole in the center. "You are familiar with the use of this item?" He passes me the pendulum.

"Yes, but in the future I'll need to be more precise about how I word my questions. Right?"

"Correct." He hands me the vial. "If you think

at any time that you have been poisoned, drink this immediately."

"Poisoned! I'm not going to accept any shiny apples from creepy old hags."

His face registers zero amusement.

"You know the fairytale—"

"Hunting a ruthless murderer is no fairytale. Take the vial."

"Yes, sir." I do as I'm told.

"This stone can help you see what is beyond the page. You are already adept at recognizing spirits who exist on this side of the veil, but some mysteries lie beyond this realm."

"Like faeries and elves?"

"Like deadly poltergeists and fallen angels."

I gulp. "Seriously?"

"Have you ever known me to jest?" His bulbous nose twitches.

"I guess not. I mean, no. I mean, fallen angels? Like demons?"

He harrumphs and smooths his mustache with a thumb and forefinger. "'Demons' is a human word. We tend to insist on labeling things we don't understand. This tendency stems from a need to either over or under emphasize our version of reality."

My head is spinning, but I somehow manage to keep my mouth shut.

"Do you recall your vision when you held the sword?"

"So, the archangel was real?"

He nods as though our conversation is as common as discussing whether we'd like beans or corn with supper. "Now, that feeling of pure light you experienced—imagine the opposite."

An involuntary shudder of horror grips me and a flash of nausea threatens to cause a scene.

"That is the thing we have come to call 'demon.' I pray you do not meet one."

"Me too," I whisper.

"And the stone will also allow you to reveal the intentions underneath the words when you examine documents." He reaches toward me with a glassy, grey stone in his palm.

An exasperated sigh escapes me. "Why didn't you lead with the decoder stone thing?"

"Being well-informed could be the difference between success and failure—life and death."

"Geez! Debbie Downer much?" I take the stone, glance at the markings carved into the circumference, and shake my head. "All right, you better skedaddle so Grams and I can discuss the finer points of my traveling wardrobe."

His countenance brightens and a brief chuckle escapes. "I shall leave you to it, but promise me you will practice the runes several more times before you retire."

"Retire? Like from sleuthing?"

Silas takes a long pause and his shoulders droop under the weight of my education. "Retire, as in go to one's room. Go to sleep."

My eyes dart away in embarrassment. "Copy that."

CHAPTER 5

AFTER ESCORTING Silas to the front door and thanking him profusely for his patience and instruction, I take the "Employees Only" door into the printing museum. I've seen Twiggy guide tour groups through here twice in the last several months. An idea is bubbling. Since I founded the Duncan-Moon Foundation, I've been getting quite a reputation as a philanthropist around town. Maybe I should talk to the local high school, or possibly have Silas talk to the director of the school board, and see if they would like to set up regular tours for students in Birch County.

Look at me, being all selfless and stuff.

I inhale the scent of old ink and let my fingers trail along the edge of our authentic Gutenberg press. I'm a big fan of books, but I don't know that much about printing. Maybe I should get Twiggy to take *me* on a tour.

Climbing the stairs toward the third floor, I can never quite stop my heart from quivering when I see the stain on the wooden tread and think about how Pyewacket took a bullet for me and my dad. My brave wildcat. Of course, that's another story.

When I reach the third floor, I pause to eavesdrop.

Grams is swirling over an antique desk, working out a particularly difficult section of her memoirs.

"Well, I'm not sure if I should 'out' Max. I didn't actually have confirmation of his affair until after I died. That hardly seems fair. However, it does make me a more sympathetic character if the affair is the catalyst that drives me to drink . . ." She taps one of her perfectly manicured fingers on her coral lip and sighs.

"Would you like a second opinion, Grams?"

She presses a wispy hand to her ghostly bosom. "Oh, Mitzy! You scared me half to death."

"Actually—"

Her eyes widen and we both burst out laughing. "Hello, dear."

"Hi. Not that you asked, but I really don't think you should use Max's infidelity as a scapegoat. You definitely had your suspicions in Paris, but it was through my work as an afterlife interpreter that you got the actual proof. I think all of us are learning about taking responsibility for our actions. If you ask me, and again, you didn't, but I think breaking Odell's heart is what drove you to drink."

She dissolves into a sprinkle of falling sparkles, like a fading firework. A sorrowful voice from the void replies, "I'll never forgive myself for that."

"The important thing is—he has. No matter what else you think about your relationship with Odell, when you mended fences at the end and he took care of you while you were sick, that pretty much righted every wrong in his book. He thinks you're a flipping saint!"

Grams zooms across the museum. "Maybe I am. Maybe that's why I can't cross over. I'm stuck here on this side of the veil to do good works, as a true, living saint."

My eye roll threatens to dislodge my peepers from my head. "I'd say there's at least a couple things wrong with that statement."

She puts a fist on her hip and stares at me. "Such as?"

"If you're a saint, then I'm Joan of Arc. And secondly, possibly less important, you're not alive."

Her fist slips off her hip. "It's that second part that really gets to me."

"I know, Grams. But we all have our crosses to bear. And mine is to endure your otherworldly input on my clothes packing for my trip to Arizona."

She claps her luminescent hands together. "Oh, I almost forgot. Are we going with a full dude-ranch theme, or are we taking it toward slinky and sexy, since you'll have Erick all to yourself?"

"Um, we're going with neither."

She lifts her chin haughtily. "Well, I say: first one to the apartment gets to choose." And with a sinister pop, she vanishes.

I turn and run as fast as my slightly thick legs can carry me. Racing through the bookshop, I ignore the "What in the actual heck?" exclamations from Twiggy.

By the time I pull the candle handle and fall, gasping for breath, into the apartment, Grams is already in my over-the-top, walk-in wardrobe.

I stumble across the carpet and lean on the doorjamb of the space I like to refer to as my *Sex and the City* meets *Confessions of a Shopaholic* closet.

With her full power restored. Grams is tossing items willy-nilly onto the padded mahogany bench in the center.

"Grams?"

Without missing a beat, she continues to rifle through the closet. "What is it, dear?"

"Can I have your full attention?"

She manages to tear herself away from a light-blue Marc Jacobs purse, which between you and me I will not be carrying, and turns toward me. "You have my full attention."

"My mom's name was Coraline. Coraline Moon."

Fresh tears spring from her translucent eyes and she rushes toward me. Her ethereal arms encircle me and she whispers softly, "Why are you telling me this today? I don't think I've ever heard you say her name. What's changed?"

Chuckling and sniffling at the same time, I attempt to gain some form of composure. "A wise man told me that it's important to speak the names of the dead lest they be forgotten."

She smiles. "Good old Silas. If he wasn't bossing people around, he'd have nothing to do." She kisses my cheek lightly and floats back a pace. "But it's only you and me now, dear. Why haven't you told me her name before?"

This is the question I never wanted to answer. I push some of the clothing aside and sit heavily on the mahogany bench. "The last time I said her name was when the cop who drove me to social services asked me if I had a dad. I said, 'No, just my mom, Coraline Moon.' To me she was 'Mom.' Her friends called her Cora, but she was my mom. As I got older people would ask about her. I got really good at avoiding answering the question. I really hated her for leaving me. Somewhere in my eleven-year-old brain I decided that if I spoke her name out loud it would mean that I forgave her." Emotions are bubbling too close to the surface, and I don't really do emotions.

Grams swirls close and whispers, "Your mother didn't die on purpose, Mitzy. Someone *took* her from you. I'll admit, I understand resentment better than I care to. One thing I learned, unfortunately too late, but at least I learned, is that a mother's love for her child transcends everything. Time. Space. Death. So wherever your mama is, she will always love you more than you can ever imagine."

We're both weeping at this point. She's leaking ectoplasm, and I've got snot running down my face. I push myself off the bench. "Gimme a second, Grams."

Heading into the bathroom, I blow my nose fiercely and splash cold water on my face. "That's really all I can handle right now. Let's get back to arguing over my wardrobe. That's a much more comfortable area."

Grams pops her head through the wall, and the sight of her free-floating hand saluting her body-less head is more than unnerving.

Back in the closet, I fight for skinny jeans and

T-shirts, while Grams is insisting on dresses and high heels.

"Look, I'm going to Arizona to solve my mother's murder. I'm going to be trudging all over the place, and it's going to be incredibly hot—"

She looks over the pile of clothes. "We're going to need shorts, dear. And you should probably take some sundresses, and maybe a miniskirt or two, a camisole, sandals for sure—"

I slip out of the closet while she continues down her endless list.

Arizona in late summer. Chances are it *will* be incredibly hot, but there's also a very good chance I'll be there for monsoon season. Now, that would be magical.

My mind drifts off to a dreamy sequence starring me and Erick in a series of rainstorm kisses.

"What about this, dear? Do you want to pack one of these?" Grams is tilting a hanger back-and-forth that displays a very sexy, very tiny black lace negligée.

Clearly, she was breaking the rules and dropping in on my thoughts, instead of watching for my lips to be moving. "Um, not on your life."

"The tags are still on, dear. It's never been worn. It's not like that. Don't be daft."

"I'm not being daft. I'm being realistic. This isn't a romantic getaway, for the hundredth time."

Grams smirks. "Oh, is it only the hundredth time, not the eleven millionth?"

"Touché."

"I thought things were moving forward with you and Erick. I mean, the all-night talk session is a big step."

Today promises to be the most unwelcome emotional roller coaster I can remember since the fateful day I learned of my mother's death. "Grams, I'm not sure I can get into this right now."

"Get into what, sweetie?"

"Remember the talk we had? The talk about Mr. Right versus Mr. Right Now?"

She sighs and fans herself with a ring-ensconced hand. "Mostly. What's your point?"

"I think Erick might be the right one. The right one for a really long time, not just right now. I don't wanna screw up and move too fast and blow it like I've done a hundred times before."

"Well, you came to the right place for relationship advice."

My pacing in front of the 6 x 6 windows stops abruptly, and now it's my turn to place a hand on hip. "Myrtle Isadora Johnson Linder Duncan Willamet Rogers, you can't be serious. Having a laundry list of ex-husbands and former special friends does not make you a relationship expert. It makes you a serial monogamist!"

Something in her aura turns shadowy and she looks away without responding.

"What aren't you telling me? Because it feels very much like there's something about monogamy that you take issue with."

"It's not that . . . It's a long boring story. Let's stay focused on you and Erick."

"Fair enough. But I reserve the right to recall this witness, Your Honor."

She exhales dramatically. "So, it's a 'no' on the negligée?"

"Can confirm."

Pyewacket saunters in, from who knows where, leaps up onto the four-poster bed, circles three times, and collapses.

"Well, hello to you too, Mr. Cuddlekins. You appear to be exhausted. Care to share what you've been up to?"

He stares at me with his all-knowing golden eyes for a moment, before letting his eyelids fall closed without any attempt at a reply.

"Seems like 'no' all around." Turning to Grams, I finally remember to ask the question that's been bouncing around in my head all day. "Do you have a suitcase? Because I only have a ratty backpack, and it's definitely not going to hold all of that." I gesture to the pile in the closet.

"Before I passed away, all the luggage was in

the storage closet, past the children's books, under the mezzanine."

"All right. I'll go grab a suitcase." As I walk toward the exit, Grams calls after me. "You better grab two, and that small overnight bag for your makeup and styling wand."

"Oh brother." When I get downstairs and through the children's section, I have to turn on the light in my phone to find what, I'm sure, is a hidden door that leads to this alleged storage space.

Imagine my surprise when I find the area surrounding the hidden passage scratched to kingdom come by what I assume are the nasty little claws of Robin Pyewacket Goodfellow. I'm not entirely sure why he was trying to get into the storage space, but it feels like it probably has something to do with the luggage.

Turns out this hidden door is the most difficult to open that I've encountered since I moved into the bookshop and started uncovering secret passages. You actually have to twist a small portrait hanging on the wall and depress a button hidden beneath an embossed header strip of cloth wallpaper at the same time. If not for the intermittent aid of my moody enchanted mood ring, I'm not sure I could've figured it out.

Once I succeed in gaining access, I drag out two suitcases and begrudgingly pull out the overnight case as well. On my way back up the spiral staircase, one of the large bags catches on the edge of the bottom step. I lose my balance, fall backward, and bang my rear end and head as I land on the first floor.

The dulcet tones of Twiggy's cackle are my sole reward. "Thanks for the show, kid. Where ya headed?"

Oops. Apparently Twiggy is the only one who hasn't heard my sad story. Since she's not one for chit-chat, I'll cut to the chase. "Headed back to Arizona for a week or two. Turns out my mom was murdered and I'm going back there to find out who did it."

"Sounds about right. You want me to feed the furry beast while you're away?"

"Would you?"

"No problem. Give my regards to the rattlesnakes."

I'm sure you notice that she made no offer to help me lug these cases upstairs. Classic Twiggy.

Rather than risk a second fall, I make two trips up the spiral stairs and save myself from additional bruising.

When I roll the suitcases into the apartment Pyewacket's head pops up in surprise.

"Is this what you were looking for, buddy?"

"Ree-ooooow?" Who wants to know?

"And what would you need a suitcase for?"

He does not reply, but his bright eyes dim with sadness.

"Were you trying to hide in my suitcase? Are you going to miss me, Pyewacket?"

"Reow." Can confirm.

Striding toward the bed, I scratch his head playfully. "I'm gonna miss you too. I think I'll actually miss you more than Grams. But don't tell her, all right?"

"Ree-oow." That one sounded a bit conspiratorial.

"That's my guy."

Spinning back toward the suitcases, I come face-to-face with Ghost-ma. Arms crossed, lips pursed.

"I wasn't serious. I was having a moment with Mr. Cuddlekins."

She shakes her head. "Well, your lips were moving, so it was fair game."

I shrug.

"When is that Howie fellow coming? And how are Pyewacket and I going to operate this newfangled equipment?"

"Don't worry. He'll be here in about an hour. And I told him I needed a setup simple enough for a child to operate. So that should have you both covered."

CHAPTER 6

THE FAMILIAR BING BONG BING of the door-bell at the alley heralds the arrival of Howie Fairlane.

Walking toward the side door, I can easily imagine the appearance of a man who bills himself as the Great White North's only IT specialist. I'm picturing a decent-sized potbelly, a short-sleeve button-down shirt, definitely glasses, and, most likely, greasy hair.

Pyewacket takes up a protective crouch inside the back room, and I chuckle as I open the alley door.

"Come on—" My voice doesn't catch in my throat, it completely vanishes from the face of the earth. Either the man standing in the alley is not

Howie Fairlane, or I have gravely misjudged the information technology business in almost-Canada.

"Mitzy? Mitzy Moon?" A hand is proffered. "I'm Howie Fairlane. You called about the tech install?"

My hope is to continue nodding my head and pray for the return of vocal abilities. Howie Fairlane is not a stereotypical geek. Howie Fairlane is a leading man! If I were casting roles for a student film, this six-foot four-inch Adonis would never in a million years play a computer nerd. His close-cropped black hair, rugged jaw, moose-sized shoulders, and bulging biceps scream "on-screen hero."

"Am I at the wrong address? 'Cuz as far as I know, there's only one Bell, Book & Candle in Pin Cherry. But, I always say, you learn something new every day." He shuffles his feet playfully and points into the space behind me. "Am I staying or am I going?"

Finally! Vocal abilities resume. "Sorry, I was expecting a delivery." That is definitely one of the lamest lies in history. Let's see if I can make a full recovery. "I'm Mitzy. Pleased to meet you, Howie." I grip his outstretched hand and shake it vigorously.

"Nice handshake. A lot of women are afraid to really give it their all."

Oh brother, I sincerely hope Howie is not a male chauvinist pig. That would seriously spoil my ogling. "Well, come on in. Like I said on the phone, I need a super-simple set up with, kind of, a one-button activation. Can you do that?"

"If Howie Fairlane can't do it, nobody can."

His cheesy smile and forgettable tagline almost ruin the view. Almost.

At the bottom of the spiral staircase, I turn and hold up one finger. "Can you wait right here? I need to make sure the apartment is presentable. I'll only be a minute." Unhooking the "No Admittance" chain, I let it hang and race upstairs to pull the candle handle in secret. Once the bookcase slides open and I confirm that none of my unmentionables are scattered about the apartment, I invite him up. "All clear, Howie."

The wrought-iron spiral staircase creaks under the weight of this yoked beast. And for those of you who aren't hip to all the weight-lifting terminology, "yoked" means incredibly muscular—especially around the neck area. I think they're called trapezoids or maybe rhomboids? Not entirely sure.

Howie scans my digs and nods in appreciation as he crosses the Rare Books Loft. "Lotta books. I'm more of an eReader guy, when I read at all. You know, I mostly code stuff in Pascal and Fortran."

I scrunch up my face. "Fortran? Is anything still programmed in Fortran?"

Howie laughs uncomfortably. "Sorry about

that, not many folks around here have any tech savvy, so I've grown a little lackadaisical with my jargon. I usually toss around nonsense words and it leaves the 'how'd he do thats' in the dust."

It takes a great deal of restraint to prevent me from rolling my eyes directly in front of his face. I'm going to go out on a limb and guess that old Howie here is single. Let's test my theory. "So how long have you and your wife lived in Pin Cherry, Howie?"

"Oh, I'm not married. Why do you ask? You like what you see?" He leans close and flexes his pecs.

Ew and double ew. One for each unwelcome chest muscle. "Just making conversation. I'm actually—"

"*How-to* Fairlane? What are you doin' in my girlfriend's apartment?" Erick Harper crosses his arms over his own impressive chest and tilts his head questioningly in Howie's direction.

"Ricky?" Howie's tree-trunk legs stride toward the sheriff. "Ricky Harper? Haven't seen you since we won the state championships! Boy oh boy. Looks like ya took good care of yourself. Coach would be proud."

It never ceases to please me when we run into one of Erick's old acquaintances. Apparently, his mother isn't the only one who calls him "Ricky." I'm guessing it actually took the two tours in Afghanistan and being elected sheriff to *mostly* free him of that unwelcome nickname.

"It's Sheriff Harper now, How-to."

My curiosity can only be suppressed for so long. "So, a couple questions. Why the nickname How-to? And, how do you two know each other?"

Clearly not one to stand on manners, Howie jumps straight in with an answer.

"Ricky and I went to high school together. He was a—sophomore?—when I was a senior. Am I right, Ricky?"

"It's Sheriff Harper, and I was a freshman when you were a senior."

"Sure, sure. Did you know I'm still coaching? Running those kids through some of the old drills. Boy are kids powder-puffs these days!"

Erick glances at me and manages an inconspicuous shrug. "Howie got his nickname because he was always showing everyone on the team 'how to' do the drills properly. I guess you could say he was coach's favorite."

A broad grin spreads across Howie's chiseled features, and the room fills with an extra dose of testosterone. "Now, I'm the coach." He jerks a thumb toward himself. "Got my own favorites."

My eyes can no longer resist. They roll hard, and my left eyelid flutters.

Erick chuckles, but covers well. He reaches a friendly hand toward Howie and they perform some strange "bro dance." They grip hands, bump elbows, slam chest/shoulders together and pat each other on the back. It's all very manly.

"Back to my original question, Howie. What are you doing in my girlfriend's apartment?"

Howie looks from me to Erick two or three times, like he can't connect the dots between my enquiry regarding his marital status and the sudden appearance of a boyfriend.

Overcome with mercy, I ease his mind. "Like I said, Howie, I was making conversation."

His massive shoulders actually manage to sag with disappointment. "Sure, of course. Let me bring in my gear and I'll get you set up. I'll need your Wi-Fi password."

I stare at him as though maybe he just arrived in Pin Cherry Harbor. "I don't have Wi-Fi here, Howie. I honestly didn't even know they had Wi-Fi in Pin Cherry."

"Huh. Go figure." He shrugs.

I have no intention of going anywhere to figure anything, but I'm not sure what his next move is going to be. "Can you set up the conferencing without Wi-Fi?"

"You bet. We'll add a device to your mobile

plan and then you can run it through your cell service provider."

Smiling, I nod and point. "Make it so, number one."

Erick chuckles at my *Star Trek* reference, while Howie's face is a perfect blank.

"You're nothing like the IT guys I've met before, are you, Howie?"

"Not sure. I'm the only IT guy around." He flashes his eyebrows as though he's made a joke.

"Well, you bring your gear in and I'll see what Sheriff Harper needs. Sound good?"

"I'm on it." He hustles back downstairs, and when the alley door slams it's my cue to burst out in laughter.

Erick allows himself a brief chuckle. "Take it easy on Howie. He always means well."

Attempting some of my own folksy banter, I ask, "What can I do ya for, Sheriff?"

He shakes his head. "I came over to see if you were planning on checking any bags? I can fit everything I'm taking in a carry-on, but I have to check my gun."

The tiny follicles on the back of my neck stand on end and I'm instantly reminded of the potential seriousness of our investigation. "You're taking a gun?"

He nods. "I know it's been a decade, but the

kind of people who cover up a murder by staging an accident aren't generally real cooperative with investigations. I'd rather be safe than sorry."

"Copy that." I gesture to the two large suitcases on my bed. "I'm definitely checking some bags."

He leans back and laughs. "Wow. I wasn't aware I was traveling with such a diva."

"Take it easy. It's not my idea. Grams—"

"For a girl who never met Isadora Duncan when she was alive, you sure do seem to know a lot about her." Erick sizes me up and grins.

When in doubt, lie it out. "If you would've let me finish, I was going to say that Grams left me all this luggage, and it kind of felt disrespectful not to use it. Plus, I need to pack a couple of disguises, in case I have to go undercover."

"Trust me, Moon, that's not happening."

"You're not the boss of me."

"Don't I know it." He sighs and nods. "I'll pick you up at five, and that's a.m.—0500 hour. I know the guy at the local airport, so we only need to get there an hour early instead of two. Did you print out the tickets?"

"No. They're in my phone."

"Fair enough. But cell service is spotty out at the airport, so be sure to download a PDF to your phone in case we can't get a signal out there."

I cross my arms stubbornly. "I was already planning on doing that."

He pulls me close and leans down, bringing his lips incredibly close to my left ear. "Far be it from me to tell Mitzy Moon what to do."

"Hey! Whoa! You guys need a room?" Howie laughs uproariously at his joke and pretends to cover his eyes.

Erick lets his arm linger around my waist. "See ya tomorrow morning, Moon."

"See ya in the morning, Sheriff."

He gestures to all the equipment that Howie's carrying. "Do I even want to know about this?"

I shake my head firmly. "You do not."

He tilts his head in that adorable way that insinuates he's tipping a hat and disappears down the stairs.

Despite his gregarious personality, Howie Fairlane is an incredibly locked-on computer nerd in disguise. In less than an hour, he's added the device to my phone plan, set up the videoconferencing station, and programmed everything to a one-click activation.

I place a test call from my phone and Howie answers it in seconds. Impressed with his speed and finesse, I thank him profusely for his expertise and gladly pay his invoice.

He's surprisingly self-deprecating as he gathers up his tools and a few spare parts.

As soon as he exits the bookstore, Pyewacket appears.

"Are you ready to learn how to use the latest internet phone and online meeting service, Phoom?"

"Reow." Can confirm.

And now I'm teaching a cat how to answer the Phoom! Seeing ghosts is starting to seem normal.

CHAPTER 7

IN CASE YOU'VE FORGOTTEN, I hate mornings
more than a certain orange-tabby cartoon cat. However, the prospect of spending more than a week
alone with Sheriff Too-Hot-To-Handle has helped
me turn my frown upside down.

My bags are packed.

My fiendish feline has been fed.

My hair is style-adjacent.

My T-shirt is appropriately snarky.

Funny you should ask . . . It's a heather-grey tee
featuring an angry cat beside the quote, "Thou shalt
not try me. *Mood* 24:7."

If it weren't for the sniffling and tears of Ghost-
ma, it would be an almost perfect morning.

"You have the videoconferencing set up,
Grams. You can call me anytime. Of course, I might

not be able to answer every single time, especially if I'm in an airplane at thirty thousand feet, but it's not like I'm leaving forever."

She sighs dramatically. "What about the case? How will you solve the case without our help?" She gestures to herself and Pyewacket. "And what about your murder wall? You're the one who always mentions how important it is." She swirls around the rolling corkboard where I organize my suspects and trace out their connections with green yarn.

"You and Pye are a phone call away, or a Phoom, whatever that means. And I'm sure I can tape some things to the wall in my hotel room. I'll be able to call you every night, from the privacy of my room, and update you on the case. If you and Pyewacket have any insights, there'll be ample opportunities to share them."

She zooms toward me and envelops me in a mist of energy that's meant to be a hug.

"Sorry, dear. I'm so stressed out I can't seem to take corporeal form."

"No problem. Erick will be here any minute, and the last thing I need is for him to see me hugging a ghost."

BING. BONG. BING.

We shout in unison, "He's here."

Hurrying downstairs, I leave the chain unhooked and let him in.

He glances at my empty hands. "Would you like me to bring down your suitcases?"

Smiling, I attempt to pretend I hadn't thought of that. "Oh, would you? That would be swell."

His shoulders bounce with laughter as he walks upstairs to retrieve my bags. A few moments later, a shout echoes from above. "Just the large bag?"

"And the backpack on the settee." Despite Grams and her tendency to over pack, I managed to fit everything into one checked bag. I'm taking my old rucksack, mainly for sentimental reasons. I touch my mom's dreamcatcher necklace hanging around my neck and whisper, "I'm going to set things right, Mama. I promise."

Erick navigates the winding staircase with no problems and even remembers to hook the chain.

"Twiggy would be so proud."

"Have you got someone to look after the cat?"

"Yeah, she promised to check in on him on her days off. The rest of the time she'll be here anyway."

I step out of the bookshop and hold the door for Erick. "Where's the squad car? Whose Nova is this?"

"I parked the squad car in front of the station. Didn't feel right to leave it sitting in the airport parking lot for two weeks."

"Two weeks? I'm sure we can crack this case in a week, Sheriff."

He loads my luggage into the trunk. "The sooner we solve the case, the sooner we'll really be on vacation."

He holds open the passenger door and smiles.

Now that he says it out loud, it puts a strange spin on things. When we were traveling to Arizona to solve a murder and he offered to come along as protection, I didn't really think much of it. But the idea of taking a couples' vacation . . . That feels like a very different step.

"Are you waiting for me to load you in the car myself?"

"What? Oh, no. I was running through my mental checklist, you know, making sure I didn't forget anything."

He chuckles. "Based on the size of your suitcase, I'd say you've got everything."

Erick drives his Nova with a decidedly more aggressive edge than when he's behind the wheel of his police cruiser. Accelerators are stomped on take-off, brakes are applied at the last moment, and corners are taken at a relatively high speed. I'm not sure if this version of Mr. Driver is adorable or terrifying. Either way, we arrive at the local airport in less than twenty minutes.

Did I know there was an airport south of town? I did not. When I made our flight reservations and accepted a ticket package with a layover in Chicago, did I fully understand that the first leg of our journey would be on a plane roughly the same size as the car I'm now riding in? I did not.

But I'm an adventurous young woman, so I keep all this information to myself, shoulder my knapsack, and follow the "worn in all the right places" jeans of Erick Harper into the tiny terminal.

"Hey, Sheriff. Where ya headed?" The security officer gives a friendly wave.

I continue to forget how small this town actually is. Everyone is super cool about Erick traveling with a firearm and they have no problem with him tossing the hard case inside my suitcase.

"Keep your ears on in Chicago, Sheriff. You have the only key to that gun case and those big-city luggage inspectors don't know you as well as we do. If you hear your name over the intercom you gotta hustle down there with your key, or your gun won't fly."

"Thanks, Eddie. I'll keep my ears on." Erick smiles and we take our seats in the lobby. He places a brown paper bag between us and the heavenly scents wafting upward make my mouth water.

"I thought I smelled something in the car. Is this what I think it is?"

He chuckles. "You didn't think Odell would let you leave town without one last breakfast, did you?"

"Remind me to get him a 'World's Best Surrogate Grandpa' mug for some holiday or other." Without waiting for an invitation, I dive into the bag and grab one of the to-go boxes. I pop open the lid and inhale deeply. There it is, my favorite breakfast, and Odell even remembered to include a little container of Tabasco sauce for me.

Erick hands me a fork and the next several minutes are consumed by our consuming.

"I got so excited, I forgot to say thank you. But, thank you. I think getting this trip off on the right foot will make my first flight all the more memorable."

My companion goes completely still. The only thing moving is a tiny trickle of syrup on the left side of his mouth.

Without thinking, I lean forward and kiss it off of his face.

He blushes, looks down, and wipes his mouth with a napkin. "Do you mean first flight on a small plane?"

"Nope. I mean, inaugural flight. I mean, literally the first time this body will be that far above ground."

He grins nervously. "And you're not worried?"

"Should I be? I mean, planes have been flying since the Wright brothers, right?" I shoot him a wink.

"Not the best example, since their first flight

ended in a crash. But if you're cool, calm, and collected, then I'm happy to hear it."

Tilting my head, I ask, "Are you a nervous flyer, Sheriff?"

"I used to be. But after you parachute out of a bunch of planes and speed-rope from a few helicopters, you get over it real fast."

"Wow, I didn't realize I was flying with an expert." Finishing the last of my home fries, I offer to take Erick's empty container to the trash with mine. By the time I return, we're called to board.

"Have a safe flight, Sheriff." The gate attendant smiles and waves us through. And by us, I mean Erick and myself. We are the sole passengers on North by Northwest flight number seventeen.

The plane has four seats on each side of the aisle. Erick chooses row two on the left side of the plane, and I choose row two, right side of the plane.

As the aircraft careens down the runway he reaches across the gap and grips my hand. "Here's to your first flight, Mitzy Moon."

The crazy floating feeling in my stomach, as the plane lifts off the ground, is honestly more unnerving than I expected.

Even his adorableness barely makes it tolerable.

Unfortunately, moments after we're airborne, our pilot, who I can see through the open cockpit one row ahead of us, announces over an intercom that we should expect turbulence on our flight to Chicago.

Not one to disappoint, he delivers said turbulence a heartbeat later.

That delicious breakfast that I was so pleased to devour back down on terra firma is having a severe dispute with my innards.

"Um, Erick?"

"Yeah, what's up?"

"I think I'm gonna be sick. Where's the restroom?"

His eyes widen and he shakes his head. "There is no lavatory on these puddle jumpers. See that little sack in the seat pocket? That's your 'receptacle'."

I glance down at what appears to be a white coffee bean bag, complete with metal tabs to seal in whatever gift I deposit, and shake my head. "No. No. I can't throw up in front of you."

He takes my hand and lays three fingers on my inner wrist. "Let's hope you don't have to. Close your eyes and take some deep breaths, while I see what I can do about making this motion sickness disappear."

I close my eyes, but I'm afraid if I breathe deeply my exhale will expel more than either of us bargain for. So, I take shallow breaths as Erick uses his thumb to firmly massage a little spot between the two tendons. I have no idea what's happening. "What are you doing?"

"It's called acupressure. We used to teach it to the newbies on their first drop. You can't take motion sickness meds when you're getting tossed into a hot zone. So this was the next best thing."

I'd heard the term acupressure bandied about by many of the woo-woo crystal crunchers in Sedona, but I never expected to have to rely on it to save my dignity. "You can't be serious? This really works?"

"Cross my heart and hope to—"

"Do not finish that sentence on an airplane, Erick Harper."

His big blue eyes fill with mirth. "10-4." He continues to massage the little acupressure spot on my wrist and I have to admit to a diminishing of my nausea.

By the time we skitter to a rough landing in Chicago, I'm more than ready to get off this flying lunch box. However, I am also pleased to report that I did not toss my cookies in front of my boyfriend.

Oh, and my insides get a little swoony when I realize that he held my hand, and massaged my wrist, for the entire flight.

We deplane and find a comfy spot to hole up during our extended layover. And despite our ears perking up every time the intercom goes off, Erick isn't called to open his gun case.

When first-class passenger boarding is called for North by Northwest's Dreamliner 787 flight to Phoenix, I jump up and grab my backpack.

Erick hooks a finger through one of my belt loops and smiles. "Easy, Moon, that's first-class boarding. The steerage, like you and me, get to fight it out in about twenty minutes."

I slowly unhook his finger from my belt loop, drop his hand in his lap, and put a hand on my hip. "Guess what, Harper? You got bumped up to first class today."

His eyes register concern and his brow furrows. "Hey, we talked about letting me pay for things, remember?"

"Oh, I remember. But this is *my* first flight. And I'm allowed to celebrate it in whatever way I choose." I grab his hand and pull him to his feet. Trying to ignore all the tingles, I hand him his carry-on and put a little *extra* in my wiggle as I make my way toward the attendant standing by the boarding gate.

"Hello. Mitzy Moon and Erick Harper checking in for the first-class suite."

Her suspicious gaze instantly transforms to eagerness to please as I hand her my phone with the boarding pass images. She scans our tickets and escorts Erick and me down the jetway. "The attendant at the door will take you to your suite, Miss Moon. Please let him know if you and your guest require any champagne."

Glancing over my shoulder, I give Erick a sly wink. "That sounds divine."

A muffled chuckle erupts from my traveling companion.

The next flight attendant practically bows as we board the plane and immediately sweeps Erick and me up a staircase to our private, first-class suite.

"Could we get a bottle of champagne?"

"Right away. Is Veuve Clicquot acceptable, Miss Moon?"

Erick's eyes are as wide as saucers.

"I suppose." I'm barely able to contain my snickering until the attendant leaves.

Tossing my raggedy rucksack on the huge sofa, I grin. "Little different than speed roping out of a helicopter, eh, Sheriff?"

He walks past me and looks into the second compartment of our suite. "There's a bed in here." He turns and looks at me. "Like a person could lie down flat and sleep." He shakes his head.

Sitting on the surprisingly comfortable sofa, I grab a chocolate-chip cookie from the tray. "I could definitely get used to this."

He sits next to me and lets out a low whistle. "You and me both, Moon. You and me both."

The flight attendant returns with our champagne—on ice. He shows us where the temperature controls are for our suite, and let's us know he'll be returning in about thirty minutes for our lunch order.

As soon as he leaves, we both giggle like schoolchildren.

"All right, I'm over it. Now I just feel silly."

Erick grins. "Me too. Can you imagine what Paulsen would say?"

"Sorry to disappoint, but the last person I want to talk about right now is Pauly Paulsen."

He smiles knowingly. "Seriously, though, this is pretty over the top. Wouldn't it have been enough to sit in first class?"

"I'm glad you asked that. I toyed with the idea of sitting in first class, but we're going to be in the air for several hours and I thought it would be a good time to go over the case and plan our strategy. I didn't want any snooty passengers dropping eaves."

He nods. "Well then, it seems like you definitely made the right choice." Raising his glass he declares, "To Mizithra Achelois Moon! Ruler of all she surveys!"

CLINK!

We entwine our arms, struggle to sip bubbly out of our glasses, and share a fresh round of giggles.

I'm beginning to wonder how much planning we'll accomplish while imbibing French champagne at thirty thousand feet—

The captain's voice comes over the intercom with pertinent updates.

Correction, thirty-five thousand feet.

CHAPTER 8

TURNS OUT, our actual in-flight checklist looks something like this: 1. Consume inordinate amounts of French bubbly: CHECK; 2. Read through case files and plan our investigation: _____.

I think we can all see where I went wrong. The upside is, a Dreamliner 787 flies a lot more smoothly than a de Havilland Devon 8, so there is no repeat motion-sickness incident.

I've decided to declare the Chicago/Phoenix leg of our journey as my official first flight.

Even though it's been less than a year since I ran out on my underwhelming life in Arizona, I'd already forgotten the heat.

As Erick wheels my bag toward the rental-car counter he licks his lips desperately. "It's such a dry heat here. It kind of reminds me of Afghanistan, but not in a good way."

I would never make light of his service to his country, but his comment begs the question, "Are you saying that you actually have good memories of Afghanistan?"

He shrugs. "Fair question, but, yeah. Obviously the guys I served with were like brothers to me, so there's that, but there were also a few times when we actually got leave and had the opportunity to enjoy local food and meet the people we were protecting. I won't wax poetic or political. There's a saying about 'war being hell' for a reason. But there'll always be a warm place in my heart for those local people who welcomed and supported us."

Nodding silently, I step into the serpentine queue in front of the counter. We've talked about the guys he lost over there before and it was a difficult discussion for both of us. Now that my feet are on the ground in the desert, the emotions surrounding my mother's untimely death are bubbling too near the surface. I can't risk engaging in any heartfelt banter right now.

The line moves faster than I would've imagined, and by the time we get to the front and the clerk hands me the keys to a convertible Mustang, Erick is all smiles.

He pushes his driver's license and his credit card across the counter. "Hey, buddy, I'm definitely going to need you to add me on as an additional driver."

Chuckling, I place two fingers on the keyring and slide it across the counter toward the adorable man-boy. "I have no problem with a chauffeur, Sheriff."

The clerk's eyes immediately snap up and he looks back and forth between Erick and me. "Excuse me, are you law enforcement, sir?"

"From out of state. We're just visiting Arizona."

"Oh, well, welcome to the Grand Canyon state, sir. We support our law enforcement and would be happy to offer you our law enforcement discount. Do you have your badge, sir?"

I pretend to rub my forehead so that I can roll my eyes behind my hand. This punk kid is reciting his speech as though he's reading it off a painfully slow teleprompter.

Fortunately, Erick is a far more patient human being than me. "Thanks." He opens his wallet to reveal his badge and pushes it toward the attendant.

The clerk gazes at the badge. "Birch County? What state is that, sir?"

My shoulders sag and I can feel my feet getting ready to run.

Erick smiles. "That's on a need-to-know basis, son. You don't need to know."

The color drains out of the poor lad's face. "Of course, sir. I'm sorry."

My psychic senses catch a dose of Erick's suppressed amusement.

He spins the keys back and forth around the index finger of his left hand while he waits for the young man to make the addition.

"All set, sir. I've applied the discount and given you an extra day, for free. Please, enjoy your stay in the great state of Arizona." His poorly delivered, monotone speech finally comes to an end and he shuffles through some papers on the counter. "Will you be needing a map, sir?"

And I've officially come to the end of my rope. "I used to live here, kid. I got this."

"Yes, ma'am."

As we walk away from the counter, Erick's snickering begs to be addressed. "I'm not sure what you find so amusing, Harper. That kid called me ma'am. He's probably like a year younger than me. Ma'am! Wait till I tell—"

Erick leans toward me. "Your cat?"

I whisk his comment away with a flick of my wrist. "You don't know me."

After he backs the Mustang out of the parking

space, he romps the accelerator a couple of times. "Listen to that beauty purr."

"If you say so."

"Oh, I do. Now, will we be staying at the Ritz-Carlton or did you buy a house?"

"Rude." I exhale and select a vague response. "We're staying at a decent hotel in a nice neighborhood." I tap the information into my phone and swipe up the GPS.

Everything's going swimmingly until we get our turn at the concierge desk. She runs a perfectly manicured finger down the screen. "Miss Moon— Miss Moon— Are you sure it's for this location? We do have three hotels in the Phoenix Metro area."

Without verbally answering, I flick through my email confirmations and call up the one for the hotel. Turning my phone toward her, I smile in what I will admit is a "mean girl," not actual, smile.

"Oh, the reservations are under Harper."

Seems very 1950s to put the reservation under the man's name even though the woman is paying, I want to say.

She taps her collagen-injected lips with her teal-blue nail. "Oh dear."

Erick gives me a little nudge with his hip and moves in front of the woman. "What seems to be the problem?"

When she looks up from her screen and sees his

handsome, smiling face staring back at her instead of my frowny lips, she seems very pleased. "Oh, you must be Mr. Harper."

He gives her that crooked grin that always makes me want to confess all my sins and even some I haven't committed and says, "I don't think they're paying you enough."

"Oh, thank you. I'm so sorry to report that we only have the one room left."

My pulse races and I'm desperate to avoid the prospect of spending two weeks in a hotel room with Erick. I'm not that strong, all right! I want to take things slow. I want to do it right this time. But if I have to see that gorgeous man with a towel wrapped around him for the next fourteen days—even the Virgin Mary would lose control.

Erick must sense my frustration. "Well, that is a problem. Are you sure you can't move anything around?" He lets his wallet *accidentally* fall open on the desk and her eyes flick to his shiny gold badge.

"It's just that— I can't cancel other reservations. I could get fired."

He casually closes his wallet. "Nobody wants that to happen. But you must have a suite or something that you keep on hold in case a VIP guest shows up. Since someone here bungled our reservation . . . I was hoping"—he leans down on the counter and his citrus-woodsy smell wafts over the counter—"there was something you could do for me?"

She blushes and giggles. "Well there's . . ." She leans closer to him and my fist involuntarily clenches. "I'm not supposed to say anything, but there was a rumor that Jennifer Lopez might be checking in this weekend. But, you know what, I'm sure it's an internet hoax. I'll put you in the Frida Kahlo suite."

Erick smiles pleasantly. "I sure do appreciate it. If J-Lo shows up, you let us know."

She gasps. "We're not allowed to talk about our VIP guests. I could get fired."

I don't even bother to cover my face as I roll my eyes.

"How many keys will you be needing, Erick?"

He steps back, slips an arm around my shoulders, and replies, "Two should be enough."

She manages to simultaneously smile flirtatiously at him and glare at me. Girl's got skills.

On the nineteenth floor we soon discover that while the Frida Kahlo suite is enormous, it only has one bedroom. However, there is a pullout sofa, which Erick assures me will be more than adequate for his sleeping needs.

Well, this day has been nothing if not interesting.

"You unpack and take first crack at the shower. I need to make a few phone calls and touch base with my contact at the Maricopa Sheriff's. It's always good to let the locals know you're in their jurisdiction."

I nod and drag my large suitcase into the bedroom. As soon as I hear his voice on the phone, I close the bedroom door and dial headquarters back in Pin Cherry. The camera on the other end bursts to life and, to my deep satisfaction, I can actually see Ghost-ma swirling back and forth.

"Grams! I can see you!"

She freezes with an arm in frame. "Mitzy, I hear you. I can't see you though. I think Pyewacket turned off the camera thingy when he answered."

I glance down at my phone. "No, it's me. Hold on." Tapping the camera access on my phone, I'm rewarded with Grams' gleeful gasp.

"Ah, you lived."

"What? You didn't expect me to survive the flight?"

"I know it sounds strange, dear. I've flown hundreds of thousands of miles. But I don't trust a huge piece of metal up in the air. I'm so glad you're safe."

"I better go. Erick's in the other room, and I don't want him to catch me talking to a ghost."

"Ree-oow." A gentle reminder.

"And a cat."

"He's in another room? You mean you and Erick have separate rooms?"

"Not exactly . . . I don't have time to explain. I'll call you later."

"But you didn't pack the—"

A knock on the bedroom door causes me to hit "end" rapidly.

"Come in, I'm decent."

"Hey, are you gonna shower?"

"Um, no. Is that bad?"

"Not at all. I didn't have time to shower before we left this morning and wanted to freshen up for dinner."

"Go ahead." I attempt to gesture nonchalantly toward the massive marble en suite. "I'll watch something on TV."

He didn't have time to shower? I risk a whiff of my own post-travel aroma and shake my head with disappointment. He smells that delicious without a shower? Oh brother, this is going to be the longest two weeks of my life!

CHAPTER 9

THE DAWNING of our first morning in Phoenix brings a mixed bag of emotions. The time has come for me to face the truth about my mother's death. Whatever stories I told myself to keep from disappearing into sorrow, it's time to put on my big-girl pants and solve a murder.

Glancing out the passenger window, I catch my reflection in the sideview mirror. I stare into the reflection's soft grey eyes and whisper wordlessly, "I'm on the case."

Erick dices in and out of the insane traffic of downtown Phoenix as though he's channeling Mario Andretti.

The patient, automated voice of the GPS keeps him company, while my eyes glaze over and drift toward the blurring scenery. Nothing looks familiar.

No part of the country's fifth-largest city offers me any welcome. Wherever my mother and I lived, whatever local haunts brought us comfort, they are either gone or simply erased from memory.

"Did you make a list of questions?"

Erick's thoughtful words pull me back to the task at hand. "I'm kind of a seat-of-the-pants girl, in case you haven't noticed."

He smiles. "Maybe you should let me do the talking."

"Why? I can think on my feet."

"No argument here. But unsolved cases are a sensitive subject, and sometimes you maybe speak before you think." He swallows and stares straight ahead.

"Are you trying to say I'm hotheaded, Sheriff?"

"No judgment. I'm trying to get things off on the right foot. If we're going to get anywhere with a decade-old murder case, we're going to need cooperation. I'm just saying that, of the two of us, I feel I can be more diplomatic. Again, no judgment."

"It feels a little judge-y."

He chuckles. "But—"

"But, you're not wrong. I'll let you do the talking while I search for other clues."

He turns into an underground parking garage, flashes his badge, and we're granted access.

The lobby of the Phoenix Metro PD is a far cry from the "Sheriff Valenti meets Andy Taylor" warped wood paneling of the Pin Cherry sheriff's station.

"Sheriff Erick Harper here to see Detective Vianca Delgado." Erick places his badge and ID on the counter.

The civilian liaison—I'm just reading her badge—barely glances at the identification. She picks up the phone, taps in a four-digit extension, and announces our arrival.

"Waiting area is over there." She gestures to a bank of uncomfortable chairs, half occupied by other forgotten souls. "Have a seat. Delgado will be down."

Erick slips his identification back into his pocket and nods politely. "Thank you."

I'm starting to see what he meant. I think I would've gone with, "Thank you, soooo much," in a rather snotty, implicitly ungrateful tone.

We barely have a chance to experience the discomfort of the furniture before the elevator bell dings, and an all-business detective walks toward the herd of chairs. "Don't take this the wrong way, but you two look like out-of-towners. I'm Detective Delgado."

Erick is instantly on his feet, offering her a warm handshake. "Nice to meet you, Detective.

Sheriff Erick Harper, although I'm not here in any official capacity."

She offers a genuine smile and tucks a lock of her wavy black hair behind her ear. "The email from County Sheriff's said you were looking into a cold case?"

He smiles and gestures for me to join the awkward triumvirate. "Yes, thanks. Let me introduce Mitzy Moon. We're looking into her mother's death, roughly eleven years ago."

Delgado offers me her hand and I shake it as politely as possible. "Hi. Thanks."

"I'll do what I can. But that was before I joined the force." She pushes a hand in the pocket of her jeans. "Let's get started by pulling the files, and I'll try to put you in touch with whoever was the lead on the case. Sound good?"

Erick nods and generously offers her additional smiles. "Sounds great, Detective."

She turns and we follow her to the elevator.

Once inside, she presses the button marked "B" and the elevator descends into the bowels of the building.

When the doors open she confidently strides out and talks as she walks. "Technically, the records should still be here. Anything over twenty years is stored off-site. We're in the process of scanning everything into an electronic database, but it's more difficult and time-consuming than it sounds—especially with physical evidence. But let's not get ahead of ourselves."

Erick nods and I glance down at my useless mood ring. I sure hope this thing plans on working overtime during this investigation. No one seems too positive about our odds of solving such an ice-cold case.

Delgado taps her ID badge and the officer on the other side of the bulletproof glass presses a button.

A voice crackles through the speaker above the window. "Please remove your ID badge, place it in the drawer, and standby for verification."

Delgado unclips her photo ID from the placket of her white button-down shirt and follows the procedure. Her badge remains on the waistband of her slim-fit jeans.

Once the particulars have been handled, we're given a form to complete.

"You need to fill this out. We'll submit the request and the records should be pulled in two to three days."

I immediately start shaking my head.

Erick places a hand on my arm.

"Look, Detective Delgado, I've only got two weeks leave. You know how it is. The victim was

Mitzy's mother. It'd sure mean a lot if we could expedite the records request."

Detective Delgado tilts her head and stares. Luckily my extra senses pick up on the wave of compassion that fills her heart, but she somehow manages to prevent that emotion from flooding her intense, dark-brown eyes. She would be a tough interrogation for anyone without psychic advantages.

"10-4, Sheriff." Delgado takes the completed document, writes something in the upper left-hand corner, and slides it through the security drawer.

The officer on the inside retrieves the form, sees the note, and presses the intercom. "Right away, Detective."

She turns toward us and gives Erick a subtle nod.

He returns the nod.

I do nothing, because I don't understand their secret cop code. However, I am smart enough to figure out that we're going to get those records today —and that's very good news.

Delgado collects the single box representing every known piece of information about my mother's now-suspicious death and escorts us back to the lobby.

She hands the box to Erick and removes the top. "Let me grab that lead detective's name real quick.

I'll clear it with the chief and put you guys in touch with him, or her."

Erick flashes another dose of his Midwestern charm. "Thanks for your help, Detective. We appreciate it. You've got my cell phone number if anything comes up."

She nods, and her eyes slowly track toward me. "If I didn't say it earlier, I am sorry for your loss."

My clairsentience confirms that her sentiment is sincere, which makes it burn in my gut all the more. "Thanks. It was tough, finding out the truth, but hopefully we can finally get her some justice."

She clenches her jaw, and I know she's holding something back. But we met five seconds ago and I don't think it's the time for me to flaunt my secret powers. So, I roll with a standard, "Thanks again."

Back at the hotel, we take the lovely bowl of precisely arranged fruit off the dining table and start unpacking the evidence.

Erick is going through the box and calling out categories as he hands me the information.

"I can't believe there's only one box. I mean, there were five boxes of evidence for my dad's case, and that was over fifteen years ago."

His hand instantly stops shuffling papers. "What did you say?"

Oops. There I go, letting my guard down again. "Which part?"

He leans back in the chair and adjusts the box in his lap. A frustrated, but impressed, expression works its way through the enticing features of his face. "I suppose I'm referring to the part about the boxes of evidence. Clearly, you didn't live in Pin Cherry Harbor back when your father was on trial, and, as far as I know, there were no five- or six-year-old girls serving as remote consultants to the investigative team. I'm curious where you came up with that oddly accurate number of 'five' boxes?"

Swallowing, I make a pathetic attempt to paint my features in a portrait of innocence. "Lucky guess?"

"Are you asking or telling? Because I may not get quite as many hunches as you, but based on deductive reasoning, I'd say you've actually seen the boxes of evidence."

I widen my eyes and smile.

"Hold on." Erick grins. "Let me try my hand at this *hunchy* thing." He numbers off his assumptions on his hand, starting with his pinky finger. "You own the bookshop. Twiggy works at your bookshop. Twiggy has an on-again off-again thing with the records tech, Wayne. And somehow or another you indebted yourself to the point of being required to attend a blind date with one of Wayne's friends. Fortunately, I turned out to be that friend, but, nonetheless, you were paying-up for something." He leans forward and, for the first time, I see what a formidable investigator he truly is. "How'd I do?"

I remain silent, hoping to neither confirm nor deny his suspicions.

He leans back and smirks. "Based on your body language, it looks like I'm batting a thousand, Moon."

The idea of him sizing up my body is oddly tantalizing. "I'm sure I have no idea what you're talking about, Sheriff."

"You have a *tell*, Moon."

"What do you mean? That's impossible. I didn't tell you anything."

"You didn't have to." He crosses his arms and lifts his chin. "I think I'll keep this little tidbit to myself. It might come in very handy the next time we're on opposite sides of a case."

"That's cheating."

He chuckles. "Hardly. You're a worthy opponent. I'd call it leveling the playing field."

We are about finished organizing the evidence when Erick's cell phone rings. He grabs the phone and looks at me. "It's Detective Delgado. Do you want to see if we can meet up with the lead detective today?"

"Absolutely. I already feel like time is moving too fast."

He nods and answers the call. " . . . Yes, I understand. That does complicate matters. What did the chief say? Understood. I think Mitzy and I would like to take our chances. Can you arrange it?" He glances toward me as he waits for her reply, and his eyes are fraught with doubt.

The mood ring tingles on my left hand and I glance down in time to see a stethoscope forming in the swirling black mist within the cabochon.

"Thank you, Detective. If you can text me the address, we'll proceed with caution."

As he's ending the call, I'm unable to stop my feet from pacing. "It's bad news, right? The lead detective is sick or something. He's not dead is he?"

Erick takes the box off his lap, sets it on the floor, and walks toward me. "Sounds like this case was a huge blemish on his career. According to Delgado the guy worked on it until the day he was forced into early retirement."

"Forced? Because he wouldn't stop investigating this case?"

Erick shakes his head and exhales. "Alzheimer's. He retired three years ago and had to be moved to an assisted-living facility six months ago. Delgado said the chief cautioned that he has good days and bad days. She'll speak to the director of the home and clear our visit, but I'm not sure what info we'll actually get."

"I'd still like to go. I don't want to leave any stone unturned, you know what I mean?"

He nods. "We'll head out as soon as she sends me the address."

"I'm going to grab a couple of these witness statements, in case he's having a good day." My fingers flip through the witness statement stack.

Erick's phone pings. He swipes open the message. "Ready?"

Selecting two reports, I nod. "As I'll ever be."

Over at the Sunny Cactus Retirement Community, Erick's badge goes a long way toward speeding up the process. Once we're cleared, we sign in and follow our escort down the well-lit hallway with its bright, cheery paintings hung every three and a half feet.

As soon as we enter Lieutenant Hackett's room, his young, energetic nurse smiles warmly and gestures to the two seats she's placed near his recliner.

"Good afternoon. Please, sit down. Keith is having a rough day. He may not be able to answer your questions, but he enjoys company. Although, not as much as he loves to watch baseball on TV." She pats Keith on the shoulder. "Isn't that right, old man?" She says the nickname with a teasing familiarity, and the man pats her hand as he stares out the window.

Erick reaches out and greets the nurse with a handshake. "Is it possible for us to speak to him alone? It's about an old case, and some of the information is rather sensitive."

She nods and points to a little red buzzer on the wall, next to the headboard. "If you need anything, or he becomes agitated, press that button and I'll hurry back."

He nods. "Thank you."

She slips out of the room and closes the door.

Erick sits in the chair next to me and gets out his badge. He holds the badge toward Mr. Hackett and speaks in a calm even tone. "Thank you for seeing us, Mr. Hackett. I'm Sheriff Erick Harper visiting from way up north, and this is Mitzy Moon."

At the sound of my name Keith's head snaps away from the window and his eyes lock on to me as though he's seen a ghost. His mouth moves to speak, but as soon as he sees Erick's badge his entire energy shifts.

I can feel his fear as though it's my own heart racing and my own blood pumping.

A strangled voice escapes his dry lips. "They're trying to kill me."

"Put your badge away," I hiss at Erick.

He pockets the badge and I reach a tentative hand for Mr. Hackett. "Sir, Cora Moon was my mother. I recently learned that her death wasn't accidental. It seems she was murdered. Is that what you were investigating?"

He stares at me and places a shaky hand in my outstretched palm. But as soon as his eyes catch sight of Erick, I feel the fear grip him again.

"Erick, can you step outside for a minute?"

"Sure."

He steps out and I kneel down next to Mr. Hackett's recliner. "Sir, I know you were investigating my mother's murder. We're looking into her case, and I really hope we can bring her killer to justice. Anything you can remember, the smallest detail, could help. Did she tell you that they were trying to kill her? Is that what you mean?"

He stares at me and there's a flash of recognition. Whether there's some part of me that reminds him of my mother or something in my speech that reached through the fog, for a moment he's here.

"They ran me out of the force."

"I'm so sorry you had to retire, sir. You seem like a good cop. I'm sure you could've served your community for many more years if this illness hadn't— I mean, if you hadn't gotten ill."

He shakes his head and the thick lines in his forehead deepen. "They're trying to kill me."

"Do you mean the illness, sir?"

He shakes his head and, even as I hold his hand, I feel him slip away. Whatever piece of a person that contains their life force, their energy, or whatever new-age phrase you want to use, Mr. Hackett's is beyond my grasp. I reach out with my left hand to give his gnarled fingers a final pat, but as soon as my mood ring touches him, his eyes snap into sharp focus. "Your mother was murdered."

The firm steady voice that comes out of this fragile man gives me goosebumps from my toes all the way to the top of my head. His eyes are absolutely clear and he is completely lucid.

"Yes. I know. I'm trying to find out who killed her. Can you help me?"

The flash of lucidity passes and his dead eyes roll toward the cactus garden outside his window. "Trying to kill me."

I lean back in the chair and sigh. "Thank you, Mr. Hackett. If it's not too much trouble I'd like to come back and see you again. I think we can help each other."

He doesn't turn toward me, but there is a subtle shift in his energy.

I'm definitely going to have to call Silas. Maybe there's a way I can reach this man.

CHAPTER 10

ON THE DRIVE back to the hotel an uncomfortable silence hangs between us. For my part, I'm anxious to avoid any discussion of the potential dead end concerning the retired lead detective. However, I can't be sure what's keeping Erick locked in pensive silence.

"Where would you like to go for dinner? And before you answer, I want to make sure you understand that dinner's on me." He taps his thumb nervously on the steering wheel.

Ah, his was more of an existential crisis. "Understood, but growing up in foster care, I didn't do a lot of eating out. Maybe we should check some online reviews and pick something close to the hotel."

He nods and a brief chuckle escapes. "I'd like to

say within walking distance, but the temperature doesn't seem to be dropping, and I'm not all that anxious for a hike in this heat." He gestures to the temperature displayed on the interactive screen in the dashboard—115°F.

"I hear ya. I think the jet lag is catching up with me." Yawning, I lean my seat back.

"Jet lag? Did we even travel through one time zone?"

"Yes, jet lag. And to answer your question, Arizona is in Mountain Time, but does not observe Daylight Savings Time. So, technically, even though we officially traveled through one time zone, Arizona time is currently the same as Pacific Daylight Time, so it feels like two hours."

"I had no idea you were a chronologist." He shakes his head. "You win. How about we head back to the hotel, let Grandma Mitzy take a short nap, and I'll make a list of dinner options?"

Crossing my arms over my chest, I refuse to give him the upper hand. "Grandma Mitzy approves."

By the time we actually make it back to our hotel room, I catch my second wind and, instead of the nap, I reread the police report.

"Why don't you see what restaurants are available around North Phoenix."

Erick looks up from his phone. "So, not here, by the hotel?"

"I was wondering how you'd feel about driving past the condos where I used to live with my mom?"

He doesn't reply. He sets down his phone, crosses the room, and sits next to me at the table. "Whatever you want to do. Seriously. I said that I was here to keep you out of trouble, but I'm also here for you to lean on if you need it."

"Thanks. It's not really about the case. I wanted to drive past for the nostalgia. I didn't even re-member the address until I read it in the report." My gaze drifts toward the large sliding doors leading to our balcony. "I wonder what happened to all my mom's stuff?"

He rests his hand on the back of my chair. "I feel like that's a rhetorical question. But if you actu-ally want to know what happens to the contents of abandoned properties, or homes where the owner passes away without a will or next of kin, I can fill in the blanks."

Despite the somber subject, I chuckle. "It was a rhetorical question. But I'll definitely keep your area of expertise in mind should I require any addi-tional information on the topic, Sheriff."

He dips his head in defeat. "Should we get going?"

Quickly tapping the condo complex's address into my phone's GPS, I walk toward the door.

Erick hasn't budged.

"Are you coming?"

"Don't take this the wrong way, but if you don't pull something out of that enormous suitcase you brought, I'm going to feel mildly abused."

"Copy that." Walking into the bedroom, I shake my head. He's got a solid point. Grams will be extremely disappointed if I don't wear at least one of the summer dresses she packed. I hoist the massive bag onto the bed, unzip it, and flop it open. Where to begin? Now that I'm standing here in yesterday's clothes, I'm starting to think I really could use a shower.

"Hey, I'm going to take a quick shower. Sound good?"

There's no response. And when I turn to walk into the main room and repeat my question, the sexy outline of my travel companion is already darkening the doorway.

"Geez! Way to scare the crap out of a girl. Why didn't you just answer?"

He shrugs. "I wasn't sure if it was an announcement or an invitation."

I'm about to ignore his response, but the full implication of his words finally hits me. My cheeks turn bright red and my tummy flip-flops mercilessly. "It was an announcement." I push him backward and close the door in a slow but final manner.

His chuckling fades as he walks back to the table, and I lean against the door in a desperate attempt to catch my breath and quiet my thumping heart. Thirteen days to go.

After a quick shower, I change into a cute blue-and-white-striped mini-dress and a pair of almost-flat sandals. The shoes remind me of the endless packing debates with Grams, and I miss her and Pyewacket terribly. Hopefully there will be an opportunity for me to call them—and Silas—after dinner. I comb through my hair, fluff it with my fingers, and choose to let it dry naturally. A swish of mascara and a little lip tint, and I give myself a couple of finger guns in the mirror. "Go get 'em cowgirl."

Out in the main room, I smile at Erick's wise switch to a short-sleeved cotton shirt. Too bad I missed that "switch."

He looks up and smiles. "You look great. Now all of my luggage lugging efforts seem like they were worthwhile."

I roll my eyes. "You ready?"

He pulls the Mustang keys out of his pocket, spins them around his finger, and nods. "Let's make tracks."

When we finally emerge on the other side of rush-hour traffic, in my old neighborhood in North Phoenix, the condominium complex is unrecognizable.

Seedling trees and tiny hedges have grown into

thick-trunked shade and impressive landscaping. Nothing seems familiar. Until we park the car across the street from number 630, and a scene from the past slams into my present.

I'm sitting on top of the large red landscaping rock that bears a rough resemblance to the outline of an automobile. My mother is rushing down the sidewalk with my "Violet Parr" backpack, her purse, and two water bottles. She rounds the corner and sees me sitting on the stone. "Mizithra, I told you to wait in the car."

I'd forgotten how beautiful her British accent was. Maybe if she'd lived longer, I would've had an accent. Either way, I'm definitely seeing how I wasn't an easy child to raise. Instead of obediently hurrying toward the car, I cross my arms, and this seven-year-old version of me replies, "I am waiting on the car, Mama."

She opens the actual car door, unloads her burdens inside, and walks toward me.

She was so pretty. Her skin was pale, like mine. And she's so "put together" and patient.

She crouches next to my stone vehicle, pats the "hood" and smiles. "I don't think you've got enough petrol to get us all the way over to your school. I think we better take my banger today. What do you say?"

"All right, Mama, but tomorrow let's get me some petrol."

"All right, Mitzy. Tomorrow."

That was her trick. I remember it so clearly now. Anything she didn't have time for or couldn't afford, she promised to take care of *tomorrow* . . . until tomorrow never came.

Erick gently lays his hand on my knee. "You okay? Do you want to stay a little longer, or are you ready to go to dinner?"

At first, the sound of his voice startles me. The memory felt so real, I'm having trouble accepting the fact that I'm not seven.

He reaches up and brushes a tear from my cheek. "It must be difficult. Whatever you need, let me know. And if you need me to stop asking what you need, you can tell me that too."

I swipe the rest of the tears away and grip his hand. "You're fine. Everything you're doing is fine. I kinda had a weird memory. I wasn't prepared. But I suppose the more we dig into things and the more places we go, the more likely I am to remember all the stuff I've worked so hard to forget."

He squeezes my hand tenderly. "Yeah, memories are— They sneak up on you. It can be rough."

And now I feel we're not talking solely about my memories as much as we're talking about some of the horrible images that followed him home from Afghanistan. I rub my thumb across his hand, take another look at number 630, and slowly exhale. "Let's go to dinner."

THE BURGER JOINT that Erick chose is fantastic. Bless his little heart for understanding the importance of my french-fry-related needs. However, I don't even make it halfway through my delicious cheeseburger before I wax nostalgic. The food reminds me of Odell, which reminds me of Pin Cherry, which reminds me how much I miss Grams and Pyewacket. To Erick's utter shock and disbelief, I'm unable to finish my meal.

"Do you want me to see if they'll pack it up to go? Do you think you'll want to finish it later?"

I shake my head. "My mom's case is really weighing on me. I think maybe I need to get back to the hotel and go over the files again. There's got to be something . . . Maybe some clue we're overlooking. There's no way this guy worked on my mom's case for his whole career and left only one box of evidence. I want to go over the files again, and if you don't mind, since it's our best lead, I'd like to visit Mr. Hackett again tomorrow. Maybe it will be a *good day*."

Erick walks his hand across the table and turns up his palm.

Slipping my hand in his, I have to ask, "So it's official? You've completely jacked my move?"

He smiles and a flash of mischief darts through his eyes. "I know a good thing when I see it."

I'm unable to maintain eye contact as a warm tingle swirls through my tummy. I get the distinct feeling he's referring to more than the handholding maneuver. Once again, I'm extremely pleased to have a stack of papers to go through back in the room. Sitting alone with him in a hotel, with nothing to do, could prove highly dangerous.

As per our deal, Erick pays for dinner. And, on the way back to the hotel, he exceeds the speed limit on more than one occasion.

"You seem to be quite a lawbreaker outside of Birch County, Sheriff."

My accusation brings warm laughter. "I hate to say it, but if I actually get pulled over, all I'd have to do is flash my badge and they'll send me on my way. As long as I'm not endangering people or property,

I can probably get away with a little more than your average citizen."

"Oh, I see. You're one of the cool kids."

"Not so much. It's more about mutual respect for the badge. We all know how difficult the job is. I suppose we cut each other a little slack when we need to blow off some steam."

This fresh insight sparks additional questions. "Have you ever let someone go for speeding, just because they had a badge?"

His humor deflates and he taps his thumb nervously on the steering wheel. "Sure, and I'm sure I'll do it again. But there was one time I made the wrong choice. I regret it to this day."

"What happened?"

He rubs his stubbled chin. "I was brand-new, fresh out of the academy. I'm sure any seasoned cop could smell my inexperience a mile away. I was assigned to traffic stops, and on my third stop of the evening I looked into the vehicle to find the chief of police driving under the influence of alcohol."

"You had to arrest the chief of police?"

"That's what I should've done. Instead, I tried to play out of my league and make a magnanimous gesture, simply because of the man's position."

"Was it a trap? Did they set you up, to test you?"

"No. It was a legitimate traffic stop and he was

legitimately drunk. Not fall-down, speech-slurring drunk, but I should've detained him and performed a field sobriety test."

I interlace my fingers. "Should have?"

"Yeah, should have. Instead I gave him all the respect he didn't deserve and sent him on his way. Fifteen minutes later a call came over the radio."

"Did he crash his car? Did he die?" Erick really needs to work on his pacing. I'm tired of trying to guess the end of the story. And now I have to wait for him to find a parking space in this over-crowded, fume-y underground parking structure.

As we walk toward the elevator, he continues, "No. Unfortunately, he ran a stop sign, T-boned a minivan, and paralyzed an eight-year-old child."

I squeeze his hand. "There's no way you could've known. You were trying to fit in at a new job."

"Those are pretty hollow words to say to a grieving mother."

I nod.

"Did you want to quit the force?"

"Maybe for a minute. I don't remember that part. But I remember vowing to myself that day to make decisions based on what's best for my community, and not play favorites because someone outranks me."

"So if you pulled over that same guy today . . ."

"I learned my lesson. I've actually placed two police officers, three judges, and eight lawyers under arrest for driving while intoxicated since I became sheriff."

"Wow. Watch out for Harper's justice."

"Yeah, I take a lot of flak from the other deputies, but I want to hold everyone to a higher standard. There are times to do favors, but you also have to be ready to stand up for what's right."

"Copy that." Closing the door, I make a beeline for the stacks of paper.

Erick flops onto the couch and begins an endless round of channel surfing, while I dive into the case files. I read every witness statement a third time to check the stories against each other.

The witness statements are all very similar. They saw the car stalled on the tracks. They saw the woman struggling to get out of the car. The train came barreling down—

Even taking into consideration how unreliable most eyewitnesses can be, I find it hard to believe three different people claim to have seen a woman struggling to get out of the car when, as we now know, she was already dead.

The police report covers all the details of train schedules, drivers' names, traffic control device functionality, etc. All of the facts. But as I read through the pages and pages of information, all I feel are the emotions.

Someone killed my mother.

I slide another stack in front of me. I can't remember the specific categories we were using for the piles, but it seems like this was the one we decided to title "After the fact." The stack contains the information about the storage of my mother's personal effects—

A picture falls out from between two pages as I flip through the stack. My heart nearly stops beating.

It's a picture of me, as a child. There's no date, but I'd estimate I'm about ten or eleven years old.

Once the initial emotion subsides, I study the photograph with a film-school dropout's eye. The framing is not artistic, it's purposeful. There's no Rule of Thirds composition. I'm dead center, and the terrain behind me appears to be a brick building, but it's quite blurry. A clear indication of a long focal length. Translation, someone shot this picture with a telephoto lens.

My mother did not take this picture. Parents photograph their children from nearby. They take time and care as they frame the photo. And the child is almost always looking into the camera and smiling at his or her parent.

Based on the angle and depth of field, this photo was taken from at least four hundred yards away, possibly from a second-story window.

I grasp the photo with both hands and try to force my extra senses to engage.

Where is this? Where was this picture taken?

SCHOOL.

The single word blasts into my consciousness, and as soon as I hear it I know it's true. That brown brick with thick white flecks, behind me, that was my school. I'm standing on the sidewalk in front of my school. My mom probably dropped me off and I'm watching her car drive away.

"Who took this photo?"

"Did you say something, Moon?" Erick props himself on one elbow on the sofa and mutes the television. "Were you talking to me?"

Turning slowly, I wonder if I did speak out loud?

Before I can answer, he's across the room, crouching next to me protectively. "What is it? What did you find?"

I hand him the photo.

"Hey, this is you. You were a cute kid."

Shaking my head, I point. "Look at the photo."

It only takes a second for his law enforcement experience to kick in. "This is a surveillance photo." He puts an arm around me. "In all likelihood someone used this photo to threaten or intimidate your mother."

"My thoughts exactly."

He sets the photo on the table and pulls out his phone. "Do you think it's too late to call Delgado?"

"Let's hold off. I wanna talk to Hackett tomorrow, show him this picture, and see if it jogs his memory."

He nods hesitantly. "All right, but I think we need to be more careful. If the people who killed your mother are the people who took this picture, you might not be safe."

"Erick, that was like eleven years ago. They're not going to recognize me from some photo that they may or may not have kept for over a decade. I'm sure that after they killed my mom they destroyed any evidence that would link them to her."

He slips the photo back off the table and fans it in front of me. "I knew it was you instantly. There aren't a lot of girls running around with bone-white hair. You might need one of those disguises you packed after all."

He lays the photo on the table, kisses the top of my head, and returns to lounging on the sofa.

By 1:00 a.m. he's done all the channel surfing he can stand and turns off the TV. "Hey, you gonna go to bed?"

I still have so many papers to go through, and I feel a sense of urgency I can't explain to him. "Why don't you take the bed tonight. I'm gonna keep going through papers for another hour, then I'll crash on the couch."

He sits up and yawns sleepily. "You sure?"

"Yeah, I'm sure. You take the bed. But don't get too comfortable. I call dibs for tomorrow night."

He laughs as he walks toward the bedroom. Stopping at the door, he looks over his shoulder and plays dumb. "Not sure if I'm familiar with the concept of dibs. Good night, Moon."

"Good night."

Cut to— Words and times swirling before my eyes and my pointer finger burning from two papercuts.

It's 4:00 a.m. and I'm down to my last stack of papers. Using my fingers to do some quick time-zone math, I calculate it's an all right time to call Silas.

"Good morning, Mr. Willoughby. Have you checked on Grams and Pyewacket?"

He harrumphs into his mustache before answering.

"Well, thanks for doing that. I have a situation here and I was hoping you might have an idea. The lead detective on my mom's case was forced into early retirement due to Alzheimer's. He should've been my best lead, and now I can't get anything useful from him."

Silas patiently explains to me the mechanism of the neurological disease known as Alzheimer's. He assures me that, for many patients, a high degree of information remains within their cerebral cortex. He further insists that if I use my psychic gifts in the manner that he has shown me regarding sharing images and plucking answers as they form within a person's consciousness, I should be able to gather a great deal of information from my subject.

"Thank you, Silas. I knew you'd be able to help. Sorry if this is too mushy, but I really miss you."

Shockingly, he admits to missing me a tiny bit in return.

"Well, I can't wait to catch the bast—"

He admonishes me for my unnecessarily rough language.

"My apologies, Mr. Willoughby. I'll let you know how it goes. Let Grams and Pye know I'll call them tonight."

Hanging up the phone, I slide the last stack of papers in front of me. My vision is starting to blur, my throat is dry, and my backside is pretty much done with sitting.

Picking up the stack, I pace quietly as I shuffle through the contents. Halfway through the stack, I freeze like a statue, rereading the same paragraph twice, before collapsing onto the sofa.

Should I wake Erick up? Should I call Detective Delgado myself? No. There's nothing to be done at this hour. I'll lie down and try to catch a few winks before Erick gets up.

As I lie back on the couch, my mind races and I feel certain I'll never fall asleep. However, the next thing I know my phone rings and I hurry to grab it before the sound wakes the sleeping sheriff in the next room.

"Hello?" I look down at my phone. It's a video call from the bookstore. There's no sign of Grams.

"Pyewacket? Is it you?"

"Reow." Can confirm.

"Hey, buddy. Is it important? I really need to get some sleep."

"RE-OW!" Game on!

"Shhhh! I don't want to wake up Erick, but that sounds serious. What do you have?"

Pyewacket climbs up on the desk, holding an ad ripped from the newspaper in his fangs, and clumsily drags it in front of the camera. He's not holding it quite right and he's not holding it very still. But I can make out an image and the word "Mortuary."

The hairs on the back of my neck stand up and I gasp louder than I intended.

The bedroom door opens and a shirtless Erick

stands in the doorway rubbing sleep from his eyes. "Are you okay, Moon? I thought I heard a noise."

My mouth hangs open as I take in the tall drink of water that is Erick Harper. It's only my second peek at those amazing abs, but they have lost none of their impact.

"Gotta go, call you later." I hang up before Pyewacket can protest. "Sorry to wake you. I found something in the files, and then I got a phone call and there was a picture, I don't know—" I shrug helplessly and fake a yawn. If I keep talking, I'm bound to say something about my brilliant almost-human cat. Instead, I grab the last thing I was reading off the coffee table and hand it to Erick.

"Cremated? This indicates your mother's re-mains were cremated. Was that her wish?"

"No idea. It's not something we ever discussed. But the bigger issue is, there's no physical body to exhume. No chance for us to find any trace evidence under her fingernails, or match the murder weapon to a mark left on her body, or—anything!"

He slips an arm around my waist.

I want to lay my head on his bare chest, but there's no time for that.

"I think there's a bigger issue than exhumation, Mitzy."

"What issue is that?"

Erick points to a receipt stapled to the back of the paper. "We need to see if anyone claimed your mother's remains."

CHAPTER 12

MY TRAVELING COMPANION kindly offers to order room service while I get changed for the day. But when I walk into the bathroom and stare at my own reflection, all I can do is cry.

Regardless of the fact that it's been over a decade since my mother passed away, this new information about her murder and, now, her remains sitting somewhere unclaimed has me all discombobulated.

The kid in me made my peace with the crappy cards life dealt me. I put my head down and powered through my mostly terrible foster care experiences. I thought these new details might have shed a light on the past. Rather than clarity, all of this additional information is muddying the waters.

Turns out I had a family that could've raised me. My mother's death was no accident. Whoever killed her was most likely using me, or threats against my person, to manipulate her. The stress my mother was under . . . I never knew.

Walking back into the main living area, I stop and chew the inside of my cheek.

Erick looks up from his phone. "You're not changed."

"Keen grasp for the obvious, Sheriff."

His eyes register a flash of hurt.

"Sorry, I've got a lot on my mind. I kind of forgot why I even went in there."

He pats the sofa beside him. "What's on your mind?"

Walking across the luxurious carpet, I take a seat. "I realize my law enforcement knowledge is primarily based on the television shows and movies that raised me, but don't cops generally need to hold something over a confidential informant?"

"It's true. Most CIs have to be coerced. There are very few true whistleblowers who come forward because of their own values. Why?"

"I was wondering what my mom did? Do you think she was involved in the criminal activity that ultimately took her life?"

He shakes his head, swipes his phone a couple

of times, and puts it to his ear. "I know it's early, but I'm calling Delgado."

Twiddling my thumbs absently, I wait for the young detective to answer.

"Good morning, Detective. It's Sheriff Harper. Do you mind if I put you on speakerphone with Mitzy and me?"

She must've agreed, because he sets the phone on the coffee table and taps the speaker button.

"Sorry to bother you so early, but Mitzy's been going over the files all night and she has some questions." He gestures to me.

Delgado yawns sleepily. "That's all right. I actually just got home. I was on an all-night stakeout. So your timing was perfect. What's on your mind, Miss Moon?"

"Yeah, thanks. A couple things. According to the reports, my mom was cremated at Eastern Mesa Mortuary, for some reason, and it looks like maybe her remains were never picked up. Do I need a court order, or can I go get them without paperwork?"

"If you have the receipt— You're next of kin. Should be a no-brainer. Anything else?"

"Yeah, I was kind of wondering what my mom did to get tapped to be a confidential informant?"

Delgado doesn't respond immediately. "That

could take some digging. There wasn't any information in the files?"

"No. To be honest it seems like there's a lot of information missing. I've gone through everything, and there are no copies of her reports, and no indication of which officer was her handler. Is there any way we can track that down?"

"Sure. I guess I assumed that Hackett was her handler. But that may not have been the case. Did he give you anything useful?"

Erick and I exchange a look. "Unfortunately, he was having a bad day. Maybe next time we visit he'll have some information."

"Are you headed back over there today?"

The hairs on the back of my neck bristle and something I can't explain warns me not to answer her question, but my too good to be true boyfriend beats me to the punch.

"Yes. We're going to see about the remains and then we'll head over to Sunny Cactus."

"Well, I hope you guys find some answers. I'm gonna try to catch a couple of hours sleep before today's briefing. Is there anything else?"

Erick looks at me and I shrug. He asks his final question. "One more thing. Do you have any idea where the victim was employed at the time of her death?"

"If it's not in that file box, I'll have to run a search. Text me the Social Security number and date of birth, and I'll see what I can find in the database."

"Thanks, Detective. We definitely appreciate the help."

She yawns again. "Oh, excuse me. I'll let you know what I find out."

She ends the call and Erick slips his phone back in his pocket. "Now do you want to get changed?"

"Why did you ask about my mom's employer? Do you think it's important?"

"I'm curious who signed the cremation order. It clearly wasn't you, and I can't read the signature. I thought perhaps she had a close friend at work that she'd expressed her last wishes to. It's a long shot, but we want to follow every lead, right?"

I nod mutely and stumble back into the bathroom.

Today doesn't feel like a sundress day. Today feels like a snarky T-shirt and skinny jeans day. Yeah, I'll probably be hot, but it's the most *me* outfit I brought. I toy with the idea of wearing a wig, but I think Erick is exaggerating any human's ability to remember the details of someone they've only seen through the lens of a camera eleven years ago.

We drive to the address on the receipt in silence. What is there to say? Today might be the day I'm weirdly reunited with my mother. It's not a happy thought and it's not a sad thought. It just feels like another piece of the closure I've been seeking ever since that fateful day.

Eastern Mesa Mortuary and Chapel. It sounds as bland and featureless as it looks. There are statues of happy children playing in an empty pond, and the double doors leading into the chapel are sun-bleached and cracked.

Ours is the lone car in the parking lot.

When we walk into the mortuary offices, a small woman with dark hair pulled into a low pony-tail calmly approaches us. "We are so sorry for your loss. How may I assist you?"

Erick smiles. "We're actually here to collect her mother's remains. There was a cremation—"

The woman nods her head and presses a hand to her heart. "Of course. Do you have a receipt, or a date of cremation?"

He shows her the receipt and her eyes widen. "Oh my, this is— Well, I'm not sure if— Excuse me." She scurries through the darkened doorway and I spin the mood ring on my left hand, begging for any sign. Before my magicked jewelry can offer assistance, a robust man with perfectly coiffed, thick grey hair emerges from a back room. "Good morning. Nolita tells me you're here to claim the Moon remains. It's such odd timing. We of course store remains for varying lengths of time, but these particular remains—" He swallows nervously. "Well, I'm afraid I'll have to ask you for identification."

Erick widens his stance and whips out his badge. "Not a problem, sir. I'm sure if you double check that receipt you'll see everything is in order."

At the sight of the badge, the man's anxiety triples. Of course, I'm the only one in the room who picks up on that, but it's definitely worth noting.

He steps forward and takes a cursory glance at Erick's identification. "Understood, officer. One moment." And he disappears into the back.

I turn to Erick. "He seems awfully nervous, wouldn't you say?"

He nods. "Let's get your mother's remains and make a note to check into this place a little deeper."

The ticking of the clock on the wall becomes the only sound we can hear.

TICK. TOCK. TICK. TOCK.

More than ten minutes have passed and I'm starting to wonder if this guy ducked out a back door. I say as much to Erick, but he shakes his head.

"It's been in storage a long time. It's not going to be the first urn he comes across."

"Copy that."

As my eyes busy themselves scanning the décor, my heart stops on a painting hanging beside the exit. A small girl framed by her red braids smiles down at two brown and white puppies playing in her lap. But the thing that strikes me is the sorrowful eyes. And without warning, I'm sucked into a flashback. The furniture is different. The carpet is grey instead of its current shade of green, but that painting— That painting hangs in exactly the same spot.

There are eight to ten people milling about with white Styrofoam cups of coffee, and a small plate of stale cookies rests next to a guestbook.

As I view the room through a child's eyes, all of the adults seem tall and distant. The conversation is above my head, and the few hands that squeeze my shoulder and tell me I'm being such a brave girl belong to faces I no longer remember.

In an effort to push the limits of this recollection, I attempt to take control of what I see. I walk toward the archway leading into the chapel, and the vision continues. As I stand behind the last pew, there's a police officer leaning over my mother's casket. He seems to be tucking something into the coffin. I walk closer. Am I re-tracing my steps from a decade ago, or am I directing the vision?

As I draw near, it becomes clear that the officer is not putting something in the casket, he's searching for something he hopes is inside.

A child's voice rings out. "What are you looking for, officer?"

The startled cop turns and adjusts the belt of his dress uniform. The angry and frustrated look on his face quickly transforms into false kindness. "Hey, I'm real sorry about your mom, sweetie. But you'll be all right with your grandmother." He pats my shoulder and hurries out of the chapel.

Grandmother? Who is he talking about? If I was supposed to go and live with my maternal grandmother, how did I end up in the foster system?

Placing that question on the back burner, I put one foot in front of the other and approach the open casket.

My heart stops.

There's no body.

A photograph in a lovely gold frame sits in place of a corpse.

Of course. No one who is hit by a train is going to be available for viewing. Not that I would've wanted to view anything if it was. But the memory of that lovely picture of my mother, enlarged from a family photo she and I took for my tenth birthday, warms my heart. I wonder what happened to it?

"Mitzy? Are you in there?"

Shaking my head to dislodge the strange vision, I stare at Erick for a moment before he snaps into focus. "I think I remember the funeral."

"Good. That's good. Did you remember any-thing that might help us?"

"Possibly. There was an officer looking for something in my mom's casket. When I asked him what he was looking for he tried to hide his guilt, but he left right away."

"Was it Hackett? Maybe he already suspected foul play."

"It wasn't Hackett. This officer was very Eastern European looking. He had a square jaw and icy blue eyes."

"You don't happen to remember his name do you?"

"No, sorry." I certainly can't tell Erick about my ability to replay memories with my enhanced psy-chic powers. But now that this one has surfaced, I might be looking into it with more detail when we get back to the hotel.

The compact, barrel-chested man has still not returned.

Erick stands and rings the bell.

"How may I—" The petite, dark-haired woman looks back and forth nervously.

"Excuse us. We know it's been an awfully long time. Would it be possible for us to assist in the search?" He flashes his badge one more time.

The color drains from the woman's face. "One moment." She scoots into the back.

Less than five minutes later the short, squat man returns with a white cardboard box and a manila envelope.

Manila envelopes can be a blessing or a curse. Trust me, I know.

He sets the tall rectangular box on the counter and lays the envelope next to it. "These are your mother's remains. Will you be paying in cash or check?" His gaze slides toward the floor.

I reach toward my pocket to retrieve my wallet, but Erick puts his hand on my arm.

"Paying for what?"

"Well, there's the matter of the service, the cremation, and the storage."

Erick shakes his head. "I'm afraid you misunderstand. Miss Moon was never informed of her mother's cremation or of the remains being stored here. We received this report from Phoenix Metro PD yesterday. If there are any costs incurred, you can take that up with them." He picks up the box and the envelope, and turns toward the door.

The man shakes his head and exhales in defeat. "I suppose that's fair. She was a good employee."

The mood ring on my finger burns and I look down in time to see Pyewacket holding his little advertisement for caskets in front of the Phoom camera. "My mother worked here?"

"Yes. I thought you knew. That's why we held her service here."

My patience has run out and the emotion of seeing what's left of my mother in a small box is breaking my heart. "Look, I was eleven years old. I didn't know anything. I went to school, I did my homework, and I loved my mother. I didn't know her friends, I didn't know where she worked, I just knew . . . she was dead." That's all I can take. I turn and storm out of the mortuary.

Erick stays behind for a moment, probably to thank the proprietor, before he joins me next to the car.

"Do you want to go somewhere and talk about all of this?"

I pace angrily in the parking lot. "No, I'm done talking about everything. I want to find the person who did this to my mother and make them pay."

He nods and walks around to the driver's side of the car.

His shoulders droop slightly and then I feel a dangerous shift in his energy. "Mitzy, get over here."

The tone of his voice leaves no room for questions. I join him on the driver's side and swallow nervously.

He pushes my shoulder down. We crouch beside the car as he dials Delgado.

"I'm sorry to wake you, Detective. But two of our tires were slashed while we were recovering the urn at the mortuary. It's no accident."

My hands go cold and clammy. It's not over. It's not a cold case. Whatever we stepped in . . . is hotter than a fresh cow pie.

CHAPTER 13

WHILE I DEAL with the car rental office, Erick
fields a follow-up call from Detective Delgado.

"Delgado says we should wait in the café across
the street. It's unlikely that the perpetrators would
return. This was more of a warning than anything
else. But she'd rather we play it safe."

"What about the"—I point to the box containing the urn—"stuff." I can't bring myself to call
the ashes "mother."

He picks up the box and the envelope. "What
did the rental company say?"

"They're sending a tow truck and a replacement vehicle. It should be roughly an hour for both,
they claim."

Erick locks the vehicle and leads the way across

the street. His stride is purposeful and his eyes sweep the shadows. Halfway through the cross-walk, I stop and my mouth haltingly falls open.

He takes a couple strides before he realizes I'm not following. He turns, grabs my hand, and pulls me to the other curb. "What's going on?"

"You said Delgado told us to wait at the café across the street. But how does she know there's a café across the street?"

Erick's jaw muscles flex. "You think she slashed the tires?"

"No. I don't know. Who else knew where we were going? She was home when you talked to her earlier, so it's not like someone overheard the conversation at the precinct. Do you think she's a dirty cop?"

He shakes his head. "I don't know what to think. But I know one thing, this case is nowhere near as cold as we thought. As soon as that replacement car gets here, we're heading over to Sunny Cactus to see what else Hackett remembers."

I try not to glance at the box containing the urn as we look through the envelope over coffee and pastries. The good news is, it holds the lovely photograph of my mother from the gold frame in my vision. The bad news is it also contains a two-page invoice for the charges, which, according to the notation, my mother's family in England refused to pay.

So, that must be the grandmother the officer mentioned. Apparently, in addition to refusing to pay for their daughter's funeral, they also refused to care for their orphaned granddaughter. I'm not sure why they even bothered to fly over from England for the funeral. Maybe they didn't. I don't remember seeing them there. Maybe they simply sent their condolences and refusals from across the pond.

Erick points to the tow truck pulling into the parking lot. "I'll be right back."

I smile as I watch him jog across the street. My phone pings with a text from the rental company. I reply that I'll meet them in the parking lot of the mortuary.

Gathering up the cold box and the manila envelope, I head over to the now bustling patch of asphalt.

The Mustang is loaded onto the flatbed truck and the replacement vehicle pulls in.

Erick looks at me and shakes his head. "They can't be serious."

Turning, I see the white minivan idling and laughter grips me. "It was good while it lasted, Harper. Looks like you'll have to get your racecar driving under control. We're a minivan couple now."

He chuckles and opens the door for me. However, the sly glance he gives my child-bearing hips could be cause for concern.

We drive back to the rental office to drop off our chauffeur and head straight out to Sunny Cactus Retirement Community with the urn securely seatbelted in the middle seat.

The nurse recognizes us and welcomes us into the room as she sets up chairs next to Mr. Hackett's recliner. "I wasn't sure you'd be back. His visitors don't usually return, except his son. The son comes twice a month. Bless that man's heart. His father never recognizes him, yet that boy comes back faithfully every second and fourth Sunday afternoons." She gestures to the chairs and nods. "Buzz me if you need anything."

Erick thanks her and we take our seats.

"Hello, Mr. Hackett." I slide the photo of my mother out of the envelope and show it to him. "Do you remember this woman? Cora Moon?"

His cloudy eyes are focused on a place far away, but eventually they wander over the photograph. The moment his eyes fix on the image, I hear the words "Poor Cora."

His lips did not move, but I know what I heard. He's in there. Silas was right.

"Mr. Hackett. There seem to be a number of files missing from the evidence we picked up. There are no CI reports, and there's no indication why my mother was working with the department. Do you know where the rest of the evidence might be?"

His face contorts and his lips struggle to respond.

Erick leans forward eagerly.

In my mind, I distinctly hear the word "closet."

"Did you say closet?"

Hackett's eyes widen.

I walk over to the closet in the corner of his room and open the door.

Erick stares at me. "He didn't say anything, Moon. Did he?"

"I think so. I could've sworn he said closet."

The upper shelves hold blankets, pillows, and a plastic bag filled with winter clothes. My mood ring burns and I see the image of a box. I drop onto all fours and start rummaging through the contents on the floor of the closet. My hand hits something cardboard. I push a pair of cowboy boots to the side and slide out a moving-company box. "Erick?"

He stares at the box. "Open it."

The flaps are stiff and feel as though they haven't been opened since Mr. Hackett was moved into this facility.

There are loose family photos, certificates of

commendation from the force, folders marked with various tax years. The hairs on the back of my neck show a marked interest in the "2007 Taxes" file. I flip through the first several tax forms and nearly give up. Thankfully, I flip one more sheet. "This is it. These are the missing reports."

Erick steps toward me, and stares down at the box.

Underneath the layer of personal items, hidden within the tax folders, are the missing official documents and Hackett's notes.

"We can't very well carry this box out of here. What are we gonna do, Harper?"

He shakes his head. "I guess we'll try to tuck it under our shirts or something."

The word "window" pops into my mind and my eyes snap to Mr. Hackett. He may not be able to speak every thought that enters his mind, but his mind is still whirring.

"We can set the box outside the window."

Erick shakes his head and paces. "Maybe."

"Wait." I walk over to Mr. Hackett's trashcan and remove the half-full bag. Underneath, as I had hoped, are three or four additional empty trash-bin liners. This is a classic housekeeping trick that I learned in one of my many previous jobs. I take a clean trash liner out and hand it to Erick. Replacing the half-full trash bag before returning to the closet.

"We can load all the papers in here and slip the bag out the window. Then I'll create a disturbance in the lobby while you retrieve it. Sound good?"

His eyes scan back and forth as he weighs the pros and cons of my plan. "We don't have much choice. I'd ask what kind of distraction, but I suppose it's better if I don't know."

I shrug my shoulders. "Probably."

Transferring the missing evidence into the trash bag, I replace the actual tax forms, photographs, and personal mementos in the box. Sliding the cardboard container back in the closet, I set the boots in front. I close my eyes briefly to call up the image of the closet as I found it and make a couple of additional adjustments before closing the door.

Erick chuckles. "Not your first time attempting to pass without a trace."

I shrug and choose not to incriminate myself. "Shouldn't you be figuring out how to get that bag out of the window?"

"10-4." He approaches the window, unlocks both locks and slides it up. "There's no screen. Doesn't that seem odd?"

"We'll worry about missing screens later. Get that out the window before the nurse comes back."

He ties the bag securely, slides it out the window, and presses it up against the building.

Once the window is re-secured, I place my

hand on Mr. Hackett's tremulous fingers. "Thank you. We're going to find out what really happened."

"They're trying to kill me." He blurts out his catchphrase, but there's more urgency and I can feel his elevated fear.

"I'm going to find the truth, Mr. Hackett. Don't worry. You'll be safe here."

We leave his room and he calls out again as we exit. His tangible fear makes my chest tighten. I have to focus on my mom's case, but I can't stop worrying about this vulnerable man.

Erick continues out the front door, while I stop at the front desk.

"Can I help you?" The desk nurse glances up.

Taking a deep breath, I put all of my limited acting skills to use. I feign agitation, and choke out my words. "It's so sad. I don't— I know he's in there. Oh dear!" I throw my head onto my arm on the counter and wail inconsolably. Several nurses circle around me, one patting my back, while the others coo words of comfort.

Once enough time has passed for Erick to recover the stashed evidence, I lift my head and furiously rub my eyes to create the necessary redness. More hands pat my back as I choke and gasp, desperately trying to calm myself.

"Thank you. Thank you for being so kind. I'm

sorry. I don't know what came over me. You're all so sweet."

Continuing to mumble my thanks, I shuffle out the front door.

The white minivan is waiting at the end of the walkway.

Jumping in, I shout, "Hit it!"

CHAPTER 14

My adrenaline is pumping as though I pulled off the heist of the century! I buckle my seatbelt and grin from ear to ear. "You should've seen my performance! The nurses circled around me like moths to the flame."

"As long as you use your powers for good."

My jocularity vanishes and beads of sweat are bubbling up at the nape of my neck. "Powers? What powers? I don't have powers."

"Settle down, Moon. I was referring to the acting skills."

My nervous laughter sounds hollow in my own ears.

To his credit, Erick ignores my awkwardness and navigates our boring minivan back to the hotel, where he somehow manages to make a garbage bag full of papers look like an important package as we step into the elevator.

It takes a split second after I enter our hotel room for my mood ring to turn to ice on my left hand. I look down and see an image of a maid's cart at the same time as Erick says, "I'll be right back."

He exits the room and I shake my head in dismay. I forgot to put the "Do Not Disturb" card in the key slot.

Sadly, the maid took it upon herself to gather up all the papers into one nice neat stack, but more disconcerting than the paper stacking is the possibility that she saw something she shouldn't have.

Erick returns a few moments later. "I spoke to the manager. I flashed my badge. No more maid service. You okay with that?"

"Absolutely fine."

He grins and shakes his head. "Yeah, I've seen your apartment. But now that I know the trick about the empty trash bags in the bottom of the waste bin, I can take out our trash when necessary, and if we need some clean towels we'll call housekeeping when we're in the room." He points to the white plastic bag of new evidence. "We don't want *anybody* to know we've got these."

"Copy that."

"How about I order room service and you see

what you can do about re-sorting the original reports before we dig into this new bag."

"No need, I remember everything. As of right now I'd rather dive into the pile of freshies."

He walks across the room and scoops an arm around me. "Are you serious?"

"I'd like to say serious as a heart attack, but I'm not sure which thing you're talking about."

"The remembering. You seriously remember everything on every one of those pieces of paper in that stack over there?"

"Yeah. I mean, I was looking at them all night. It's in the vault." I tap a finger on my skull. "You wanna test me?"

"Let me put in our food order, and then I think a test is in order."

While I disappear into the bedroom to put on a pair of comfortable shorts, Erick's deep, confident voice orders an array of delicious snacks.

When I return, his eyes trail over my legs appraisingly. "Not sure if I've ever seen you run before, but that sprint out of Sunny Cactus today was impressive."

"You think." I lower my eyelids and attempt a flirty curtsy with my shorts.

He pats the sofa and whispers, "Why don't you come over here and let me get a closer look."

My spine immediately goes all tingly and my

tummy flip-flops and melts simultaneously. "I think we better stick with the original plan. Either I'm diving into the new pile, or you're the quiz master."

He strides to the table and flips through the stack aimlessly. He punches his finger in between the fanning pages. "What time was the accident reported?"

I close my eyes and access the image of the police report. "1:27 a.m., but it says 0127 on the report. I don't know how to say military time out loud."

His eyes widen. "Impressive. Let's see if we can find something more difficult." He fans through the pages with more care this time and asks, "What was your mother's blood alcohol content?"

I grin and cross my arms. "Trick question. The toxicology report was missing from the medical examiner's findings."

He thumbs through the remainder of the nearly one-foot-high stack of reports and lets out a low whistle. "Are you some kind of savant?"

Having previously heard the term in reference to an *idiot* savant, my initial reaction isn't positive. "Are you trying to say there's something wrong with how my brain works?"

"Not at all. But I'm starting to think there might be something wrong with the way everyone else's brain works. Yours seems to be firing on all cylinders, plus maybe a few cylinders the rest of us don't have."

His succinct summary hits a little too close to home, again, and I'm desperate to change the subject.

Jogging over to the couch, I plop down and attempt to kick my legs out toward the coffee table in a somewhat sexy pose. "Say more stuff about my legs."

His eyes spark with heat, and my extrasensory perception flashes red warning lights.

Erick crosses his arms, grabs two fistfuls of fabric, and whips off his T-shirt. "Two can play this game, Moon."

How do I breathe? I've forgotten how to breathe. Is my mouth watering? Oh boy! I have lost control of this greased-pig of a conversation. "I fold. I fold." I hold my hands up in surrender.

He chuckles and slinks toward me like a panther, before leaning down and kissing my lips in a way that makes me hope the food arrives very, very soon.

As if my wish could be the kitchen's command, there's a knock at the door.

Wriggling out from under my bare-chested roommate, I make for the door.

"Mitzy, hold up." His voice is stern, with a hint of warning.

His mood has shifted faster than Janus changes faces. "What's going on? You don't want me to let the food in?"

He puts a finger to his lips to silence me and draws his gun. He steps up to the door, but stands beside it, not right in front of the peep-hole like all of those people who always get shot through the door in every movie I've ever seen. My boyfriend is smart.

"Who is it?" His tone is all business.

"Room service."

"All right. Leave it outside."

"Okay, but you're supposed to sign—"

"Talk to your manager."

There is no argument from the other side of the door.

Erick waits a beat and risks a quick peek through the peephole. "All clear. I'll cover you while you inspect the cart."

The playful mood from a moment ago has been obliterated. "What's going on? Why are you being so cagey?"

"Someone slashed our tires. Someone is either tailing us or getting information from a source, possibly Delgado. Whatever you're poking into doesn't want to be poked. From now on we play by my rules. Understood?"

I stand at attention and pop a salute. "10-4."

He shakes his head and gestures for me to open the door.

Opening the door, I step into the hallway while he carefully peers around the doorjamb and checks the hallway in both directions. "Clear. Check under the cart." He aims center-mass below the cart and nods for me to proceed.

The tension is ruining the vibe, so I take this opportunity to lighten the mood. Gripping the tablecloth with two hands, I yank it with a flourish. Thank you, *Ghostbusters*. My trick is surprisingly successful and the place settings, glassware, and tapas adorning the surface of the foldout table are undisturbed, while I hold the tablecloth in my hand. "Check yourself."

He leans down and checks the compartment beneath the table. "Clear. And that's a pretty neat trick. I suppose you'll want me to start calling you the Amazing Mitzy?"

I take an exaggerated bow and flourish the tablecloth. "I think I prefer the Astonishing Mitzy."

He clicks the safety on his gun and shoves it into his "inside the waistband" holster, which fits snuggly against his back.

I push the cart in and we start uncovering the treasures. "Nice selection. I call the fries."

He shakes his head and sighs. "I never had a chance."

Taking the plate of fries to the table, I slip the new evidence out of the white trash bag and begin organizing these papers into their own stacks as I munch on french-fried perfection.

This looks like everything that was missing. All of the reports my mother made to her handler, Detective Ian Butler, and the missing pages from the medical examiner's report. It seems the cause of death wasn't quite as "undetermined" as indicated on the dodgy cover page we previously viewed. They found an unusually high concentration of nicotine in her blood.

"But she didn't smoke."

Erick licks a little barbecue sauce off his finger, from the plate of wings he's working on, swallows his food like a grown-up, and asks, "What did you find?"

"The actual ME's report claims the cause of death was acute intoxication with nicotine. But my mom didn't smoke."

"You were a kid, Mitzy. Maybe she hid it from you."

I lay the paper down and slowly lift my head. "Let's say you're correct, Sheriff. If she smoked enough to die of nicotine toxicity, don't you think she would have needed to smoke three to four cigarettes at a time and chain smoke twenty-four hours a day? There's literally no way she could have hidden a habit like that from me. Not to mention the smell of smoke in her clothes! No matter how careful you are, no one can completely disguise the smell of cigarette smoke."

"Point taken. You think she was poisoned?"

"Possibly. Unfortunately, there's no body to examine, so there's no way to verify that."

"There might be." He walks over to the table and snaps a picture of the report. "Let me send this to Deputy Paulsen and see if she can track down the facts behind these nicotine toxicity numbers. If it's as outrageous as you say, we can at least use it as a working theory."

Slouching in the chair like an angry teenager, I gaze up at Erick and plead. "Paulsen? Can't you send it to somebody else?"

"I know she's not your favorite person, Moon. But I told you before, she's a good cop."

I cross my arms and continue to pout.

He flashes his eyebrows and winks. "Did I mention there's dessert?"

. . . aaaand pouting over. "You have my attention, Sheriff."

After a delectable dessert-break consisting of peanut butter and banana bread pudding with a whiskey caramel sauce, we report to the dining table and finish sorting the new evidence.

Before long, we're able to piece together the

events in a roughly chronological flow. My mother was stopped and found to be driving under the influence. Her blood alcohol content was a mere one-hundredth of a percent over the legal limit, but she happened to work for the mortuary that features largely in what appears to be a massive money laundering and illegal drug operation. Detective Ian Butler approached her about working as a confidential informant in exchange for suspending the charges.

"The detective probably threatened to push for the maximum penalty if she refused. Her custody could've been in jeopardy." He shakes his head. "It's not pretty, but sometimes cops get desperate. Drug trafficking is so well funded, it can seem unstoppable."

I nod and swallow. The reports from my mother were given at roughly weekly intervals, according to the records we have. At some point Butler mentioned involving the DEA. However, nowhere in either batch of files is there any indication that the DEA was contacted. Dropping another stack, I exhale in frustration. "So, do you think there's another box of evidence somewhere?"

He shrugs. "It's possible the DEA came in and completely took over the operation. The police department wouldn't have any reports after that. It is kind of odd that there's not some transfer paperwork . . ." He paws half-heartedly through another pile.

"And there's no mention of the person who was blackmailing my mom."

Erick looks up. "Blackmailing?"

"Well, whatever they were doing with the picture of me. It seems like someone was pressuring her, right?"

"I agree. It's strange to have a photo like that, obviously taken with a telephoto lens, but like you said, there's no mention of coercion."

"There's also no mention of shutting down the drug ring."

He nods and runs his left thumb along his jaw line. "Ten years ago they were bringing in mostly marijuana, some cocaine and I remember reading on one of these reports . . . maybe some heroin. If we assume the operation is still mostly intact, they've likely turned toward heroin or maybe exclusively meth. Although, heroin has a much higher street value."

"What's your point?"

"I think we need to find out if any arrests were ever made or if the information your mother provided shut the operation down. If the same outfit is still running drugs, then it stands to reason they wouldn't want anyone poking around."

"So, you think the mortuary is a front?"

"Possibly."

"They cremated my mom. I don't think you can fake that. Can you?"

"Front doesn't mean fake. A front is usually a legitimate business that provides money-laundering services for the illegal businesses. Funeral costs can be very high. It would be a great way to launder money. In a manner of speaking."

"Yeah, in a manner of speaking." I shuffle through some more papers and look at my phone. "It's almost one in the morning. I don't think I can pull another all-nighter. Should I take the bed?"

He nods too quickly. "Absolutely. I'll take the couch. See ya in the morning."

"What are we gonna do about Detective Delgado?"

Erick shakes his head. "I'm not entirely sure. I'll sleep on it. Maybe something brilliant will come to me in my dreams."

I nod. Funny, I was kind of hoping something sexy and sheriff-sized would come to me in my dreams. I wisely keep my fantasy to myself, and instead offer a neutral high-five before toddling off to bed.

CHAPTER 15

THE BLACKOUT SHADES in the large well-appointed bedroom are a hair shy of one hundred percent effective. As the bright desert sun forces its way through the thin gap along the edge of the dark shade, I roll onto my back and stretch.

When my outstretched arm touches some warm flesh—that isn't mine—I nearly scream.

My whole body goes stiff and I slowly roll my head to the left. As soon as I catch sight of my sleeping partner, my eyes rocket toward the ceiling.

Erick is in bed with me.

Gorgeous, shirtless Erick Harper is in my bed.

I didn't have anything to drink last night, I'm sure of it. I certainly would have remembered inviting him into the bed. My best option is to quietly sneak out of the room and pretend to be asleep on the couch.

Nothing happened.

I'm sure nothing happened. I need to get out of here and make certain I'm the only one who knows *nothing* happened.

As I carefully attempt a silent log roll out of bed, the traitorous mattress springs betray me.

Erick rolls over.

I freeze on the edge of the bed.

His voice is husky with sleep. "Where are you going, Moon?"

Before I can reply, he sits bolt upright and immediately lifts the covers to check his level of undress.

"Nothing happened," I offer defensively.

"Yeah, I'm dressed. But you— What am I doing in here?"

"I don't know." I cross my arms and squeeze myself. "You were there when I woke up."

He rubs the sleep from his eyes and shakes his head back and forth. "Right. I was sleeping on the couch last night. I got up to use the bathroom— I must've forgotten. Then I crashed on the bed. Sorry."

I rub my hands on my arms as though I'm cold. "No it's fine. It's totally fine. I'll go order us some breakfast. You take your time." I scurry out of the bedroom in my shorty pajamas, extremely grateful that I didn't choose a T-shirt sans bottoms.

Grabbing the phone, I dial room service without even bothering to look at the menu. I place my order and hear my phone ring—in the bedroom.

I skulk back in, mumbling apologies under my breath. It's a Phoom call from Grams and Pyewacket. If I don't answer they'll panic. Hurrying out of the room, I accept the call as I close the door behind me.

"Mitzy? Did you just wake up? Did we wake you?"

"No, *Pyewacket*, you didn't wake me."

"It's me, dear. Can't you see me? Pyewacket's here and he helped me place the call, but it's your grandmother."

"I know. I see you, *Pyewacket*. Erick already thinks it's awfully strange that I video chat with my cat. Do we understand one another?"

"Oh!" She claps a bejeweled hand over her grinning mouth. "We're being surreptitious. I love a good secret. You can count on me! I'll be Pyewacket 2. Which reminds me, Pyewacket 1 has something for you."

Tufted ears appear in frame and I encourage him to get up on the desk so I can see all of his furriness. "And to let you know, as usual, you were right about the mortuary. Not only did my mother work there, but we were able to recover her ashes."

Pye's response is derailed as Grams zooms in front of the camera. "Oh, sweetie, that's wonderful news. You can bring her back to Pin Cherry. We'll find a wonderful place for her. I'm so pleased. I'm so happy for you."

Part of me appreciates Ghost-ma's enthusiasm, but I'm not sure how I feel about carting a can of ashes back home. I should probably feel some kind of closure, but I can't even bring myself to open the cardboard box housing the urn.

Pyewacket turns and stretches down to the seat of the chair to recover something, turning his back-side toward the camera.

"Excuse me, Robin Pyewacket Goodfellow, that's not your best side. Can you turn the ship around, Mr. Cuddlekins?"

He twists, and clenched between his pointy teeth is a silver toy police badge.

He dangles the badge in front of the camera.

"Consider it logged into evidence."

He drops it. "Re-ow." Thank you.

"You're welcome. I'm definitely suspecting a dirty cop, but other than that, I'm not sure what you're trying to tell me."

"Reeeee-ow."

"A warning? Are you telling me I'm right? Is there someone I shouldn't trust?"

Pyewacket bobs his head in a frighteningly human way, and I find myself wondering whether he's more cogent than some of the guys I dated. "Thanks for the confirmation. You'll let me know if you get anything more specific?"

"Reow."

"Duly noted. Now, I gotta get ready for breakfast. You take care, Pyewacket 1 and Pyewacket 2."

Grams swirls in behind the wide tan head and scratches her ethereal fingers between his tufted ears. "Miss you." She grins.

"Bye."

Smiling, but missing my family, I set my phone down and lean back into the couch.

That's when I notice Erick, posted up in the bedroom doorway, eyeing me suspiciously.

"What? I talk to my cat. You already knew that."

"Right. Your cat. Pyewacket 1 and Pyewacket 2. Two names for the same cat? Two cats? Or one cat and one thing you're not telling me?"

Shrugging, I widen my eyes.

"And not to look a gift cat in the mouth, but I wasn't aware he was so actively involved in your snooping. He suspects a turncoat too? Interesting . . ."

I nod, refusing to open my mouth. No point in saying something I'll regret. There's a knock on the door. Erick turns to grab his gun, but the voice outside the door saves him the trouble.

"It's room service, Miss Moon. We'll leave the cart."

"Thank you," I shout in a loud pleasant voice.

Jumping up from the soft couch, I walk toward the door.

"Hold up a minute. We still need to check the cart in the hallway."

Like a robot running out of batteries, I come to a slow-motion stop. "And that's why you're the sheriff and I'm a civilian."

He returns with his weapon and we repeat the search-and-clear procedure, sans the tablecloth trick.

After breakfast Erick announces his plan to run a little surveillance on the funeral home and I opt for staying in the room and continuing to go over the evidence.

Secretly, I'm hoping once he leaves, my psychic senses will feel comfortable enough to make themselves useful.

He stops at the door and his expression carries the weight of the world. "I'm taking the gun. Do not answer the door. Okay?"

"What about lunch?" My bottom lip quivers in mock terror.

"Order room service and follow the procedure." He smiles for a split second and then his seriousness returns. "Actually, don't roll the cart in. Open the door, grab the food, and secure the door. And call me to check in."

"All right, but you call me to check in, too."

"10-4. I'll let you know what Paulsen finds out."

After he leaves, I throw the deadbolt and flip the secondary lock behind him.

About halfway through my perusal of the reports my mother was filing with Ian Butler, a whole new set of players emerges. All of the initial reports pertained to the funeral home and my mother's suspicion that some of the people who were cremated were not who their paperwork claimed they were.

The hairs on the back of my neck prickle to attention. It can't be an accident that my mother's service was held at that funeral home and that her remains were cremated so rapidly.

And I still don't see the connection between the sketchy cremations and these two new suspects in Scottsdale.

My fingers tap out a rhythm on the table. Who ordered my mom's cremation? I really wish I could decipher the signature on this sheet of paper.

The stone!

With Erick out of the room, I can get out that weird little stone Silas gave me.

There are far more pockets and zippers on my rucksack than I remember, but eventually I find the inner pocket that holds the stone. Leaning over the sheet of paper on the dining room table, I feel completely foolish as I move the stone toward my eye. I rub my thumb over the symbols carved on both sides of the stone and a pulse of energy tingles in the palm of my right hand.

"All right. Here we go." Holding the glassy flint stone to my eye, I look through the time-carved hole in the center. Initially there's no difference. But as I move my gaze down the page, feelings and words bubble up like smoke from a fire.

Cover up.

Hurry.

And when I reach the signature line— *Destroy the evidence.*

I scan over the signature two more times and each time the script spells out the same phrase, *Destroy the evidence.*

Turning the paper back and forth, I want more. "I understand. But who? Who wanted to destroy the evidence?"

When I speak the question out loud, the squiggly lines of the handwritten signature disappear from the page. A moment later the steady tapping of an invisible typewriter fills my head. The letters appear as all capitals, in Courier typeface.

I—

A—

N—

B—

U—

T—

The stone hits the tabletop with a clatter.

Ian Butler signed the order to have my mother cremated, and he signed it with the sole intention of destroying evidence.

If this is the guy Delgado is feeding information, Erick and I are in a lot more danger than we assumed.

A matter-of-fact knock on the door turns my blood to ice.

I didn't order anything.

"Housekeeping." The voice is timid, by design.

The word holds no truth.

Erick doesn't make mistakes, and he was very clear about the agreement he reached with the manager. There is absolutely no way this is housekeeping.

I tap out a message to Erick, on my phone. "Someone's at the door."

His response is instantaneous. "I'm heading back."

Carefully creeping toward the door, I follow Erick's example and stand beside the actual door, instead of in front. "Who is—?"

A bullet rips through the door six inches below the peephole.

Center mass, for someone standing in front of the door.

It all happens so fast, my instincts even surprise me.

With a screaming groan, I fall to the floor.

The thudding footsteps grow quieter and, in the distance, the door to the stairwell slams shut.

Once again, my acting paid off.

I stealthily crawl away from the door and text Erick. "Ran down the stairwell."

"On it," he replies.

A few moments later, a key card slides into the lock, but fear forces me to crouch beside the sofa.

"Mitzy? Mitzy, is that a bullet hole in the door?"

Rising unsteadily from my hiding place, I nod. "Yeah."

He slams the door, throws the deadbolt, and races across the room. "Are you hit? Did they shoot you?"

I lean into him and shove down my emotions. "I used your move. The side of the doorway thing. Otherwise I'd have a bullet through my heart."

He pulls me close and I can hear his heart thudding with my normal human ears. It doesn't take a psychic to sense how upset and relieved he is.

"New plan. Pack up your stuff. We're out of this hotel—now. We don't tell anyone, including Delgado, where we're staying."

"Only cash," I whisper to his chest.

His lips brush the top of my head. "Looks like it's time to roll Pin Cherry-style in this big city. No more credit cards, no more trails. Cash only. And we pick up two burner phones. Understood?"

"Understood. But I need to let Silas know. I mean, if we're getting rid of our phones, he needs to know how to get hold of me."

Erick smiles as he loosens his hold on me. "And don't forget about your cat."

I pull away and put a hand on my hip. "Remind me to ask your mother for a picture of you and Casserole when we get back to Pin Cherry."

The color drains from his face when I mention his beloved potbelly pig.

"Don't bring Casserole, God rest him, into this." He grins and shakes his head.

Squeezing his hand I add, "We're out of here in five minutes, right?"

He nods. "Or less."

As I walk into the bedroom and flip open my suitcase to change out of my pajamas, I see one of the wigs Grams forced me to pack. Stepping back to the doorway I say, "Whoever shot through the door thinks I'm dead."

Erick pauses from gathering up the papers on the table. "How's that?"

"Well, I sort of scream-groaned and fell to the ground."

He shakes his head. "What possessed you to do that?"

"I don't know. Probably some movie I watched. I figured if they thought they were successful, they wouldn't come back."

He rubs his chin absently and nods. "That's actually a solid theory. Maybe you should wear one of those disguises you packed."

"Great minds think alike." I close the door, and within two minutes and twenty-seven seconds I've transformed from sleep-deprived Mitzy Moon, into Bo-ho chic Darla Welby.

Backpack over one shoulder and suitcase in tow, I strut into the living room.

My partner looks up. "Wow! You look good with black hair." His mouth turns up at the corner in a sexy smile. "You look good with any color hair."

I blush behind my designer sunglasses and shake my shoulder-length bob. "How do we do this? If I'm seen leaving the building with you, it wouldn't take a genius to make the deductive leap that I'm alive and kicking."

Erick leans back and interlocks his fingers behind his head.

Apparently Darla Welby has the same weakness as me. We're both incapable of keeping our eyes from darting to his momentarily exposed abs.

"Before I answer that, where did this weird stone come from? Was it in the evidence?"

Releasing the handle of my large rolling suitcase, I run over and snatch the hag stone from Erick's hand. "I was looking for that. It's a little good-luck charm." I shove it in my rucksack before he can ask any additional questions. "Now, what's our plan?"

"Leave the suitcase, take your backpack, and take a cab to—" he holds up his finger while he quickly searches on his phone "—the Southwest Bank on Camelback. I'll pack the rest of this up and load it in the van. This next part is a bit of a stretch, but if you're all right with it, I was thinking maybe we don't check out—officially. We slip out, and as far as Delgado and anyone else knows I'm still staying here."

"Did anyone ever tell you you'd make a great criminal, Sheriff?"

"It's part of the job. If you can't think like a criminal, you've got no chance of catching them."

"Copy that. Darla Welby is on her way to the Southwest Bank."

He takes out his gun and makes sure the hallway is clear before I step out in my designer boots, ankle-length skirt, and fringy, beaded halter-tank.

The door closes behind me and I hurry toward the elevator.

On its descent, the elevator stops two more times and various people board. I suspiciously eye each and every one of them from behind my dark glasses.

No one pulls a gun, and no one takes any notice of me.

When the elevator stops on the main floor, I cross the lobby with my best impression of a runway-model strut, and ask the concierge to call me a cab. I didn't give much thought to my backstory, but the voice that came out was upscale East Coast. So, not *Jersey Shore*, but more Lovey Howell from *Gilligan's Island*.

Worried that everyone is on the hunt, I keep up the accent in the taxi. "Southwest Bank, the branch on Camelback."

A couple blocks from the hotel, I realize my mistake—both of them. I didn't turn off my phone when I left the hotel. And I'm going to have a lot of trouble taking out large sums of cash in a disguise.

"I've forgotten something at the hotel. Can you double back?"

The driver makes a U-turn, and I turn off my phone and toss the SIM chip out the window.

As we approach the hotel, the white minivan pulls out of the underground parking. Time to put on another performance. "Oh my word, what I forgot must be my brain. I've found my lipstick. Forget I mentioned it. We don't need to go to the hotel after all. Back to the bank. Southwest, the branch on Camelback. So sorry. Not my morning, you know?"

The cabbie nods, and within a few seconds we're behind Erick. I dig through the front pocket of my rucksack and happily find a couple of twenty-dollar bills. When the taxi pulls into the bank parking lot, I toss them both to the driver. "Sorry for the mix up. Pretend you never saw me."

He picks up the two crumpled twenties and nods with concern creasing his brow. But not enough concern to ask a follow-up question. He pockets the money and drives away.

Striding to the minivan, I open the passenger door and climb in.

"How did you get behind me? You left the hotel first."

"Yeah, but I screwed up. I forgot to turn off my phone. So we had to make a U-turn and I tossed my SIM chip out the window. Then we headed back, but I think my—"

He chuckles. "Let me guess, your performance saved the day?"

I throw on a little of my upscale East Coast accent. "There is no shame in taking pride in one's skills."

Erick shakes his head. "You really are a carnival of wonders." He puts the van in drive and pulls out of the parking lot. "I guess we better make our withdrawal at a different bank."

"And I'm gonna have to take off this wig, at least for the banking portion of our day. I can't imagine any bank is going to allow me to withdraw a couple thousand dollars in cash without identification."

He agrees. We drive for over twenty minutes searching for a bank before he whispers, "Tell you what. I don't think there's any way to get money out of your account without showing your debit card, and you're supposed to be dead. Let me call Tilly and see what I can do."

A few favors and pleasantries later, Tally's older sister, Tilly, has agreed to transfer three thousand dollars from my account into Erick's account. We make it seem like it has something to do with some law enforcement thing that Erick needs to pay for in Arizona. There's no need to tell her we're simply trying to avoid using a dead woman's ATM card.

"Thanks again, Tilly. Please give our best to

your sister and Odell. Tell them how much we miss them and the diner."

Her bright laughter spills from the speaker. "All right. You kids better be careful down there in the desert, you know."

Erick and I exchange a wink.

"We will." He ends the call and turns into the next bank we find.

"Wait in the car. I'll grab a thousand, for now." He looks at me. "That's a weird thing to hear myself say."

"Don't look at me. I haven't even had money for a full year yet. It's weird for me too."

One thousand dollars, two burner phones, and an incredibly questionable motel later, we're confident we've hidden our tracks.

I'm rolling my suitcase into the new, subpar accommodations when my mood ring burns with the image of a blinking red light. "*Enemy of the State!*"

Erick looks at me. "What?"

"Did you check under the car for a tracking device?"

For a second it looks as though he might chuckle, but then the color drains from his face. "Wait right here." I stand in the doorway as he rolls onto his back and shimmies under the vehicle. The sound of several epithets being uttered does not raise my hopes. He slides out and shows me a small blinking device.

I wheel my suitcase back to the van. "Load us back up, Harper. I'll take care of this." Snatching the tracking device from his hand, I search the parking lot and stride toward a circa 1970s Monarch.

Purposely dropping my sunglasses next to the vehicle, I crouch to retrieve them and stick the tracking device under the rear quarter panel.

Replacing my glasses as I stand, I march straight back to the minivan and hop in the passenger side. "Handled. Let's find some new digs."

CHAPTER 16

LUCKILY, there's no shortage of seedy motels in a booming metropolis like Phoenix. Or possibly it's a megalopolis? I remember learning that word in seventh grade Civics, but I'm not a hundred percent clear on what the word means.

Our new accommodations would be thrilled to receive a one-star rating! The carpet is stained, the room smells of a cornucopia of unpleasantness, the bathroom mirror has been removed, and the toilet has no lid. There's a seat, thank goodness, but no lid.

But the true highlight is in the cleverness of their "non-smoking" room.

Allow me to explain. An overturned ashtray perches on the bedside table. On its base is a faded picture of a cigarette marked by a bold red circle with a line through it. So, if you follow me: Right side up = ashtray = smoking room; upside down = glass disc = non-smoking room.

It's so simple.

Blerg.

After we unpack, Erick makes a food and water run, while I sort through the remaining evidence.

Before he returns, I take advantage of my solitude and call Silas.

Voicemail? Weird. I can't remember a time when Silas didn't answer his phone. My voicemail skills are a little rusty, but I know he'll never stand for a text. "Good afternoon, Mr. Willoughby. I don't want Grams to be concerned, but Erick and I have run into some strong opposition. We had to abandon the hotel we were staying at, without technically checking out. We're at a new place, which I won't mention. And we have burner phones. I'll leave you the number of this burner phone. I should have it for a few days, barring any additional unforeseen catastrophes. Also, I used the stone on one of the documents I was reviewing and it did reveal some very interesting information. Quick question: If I have a first and last name, but no additional details, will my pendulum even work in a city this huge? Chances are there's more than one person with this name. Is there any way I can narrow the odds? I hope Grams and Pye are doing all right without me. I sure do miss everyone."

Ending the call, I lay the phone on the cracked bedside table.

Erick returns with a selection of fast-food options.

I stare at the array of crinkled bags, stained with grease, and frown. "Oh, how the mighty have fallen. Last night it was room service and a selection of delectable treats, today it's a heart attack in a sack."

He pulls out a chair and eeny, meeny, miny, moes his selection.

His playful attitude brings a smile to my face, and I pretend to spin the cylinder on a revolver and select my meal via Russian roulette.

"Did you come across anything new?" He grabs extra napkins.

"Yes, but there seems to be a gap in the reports. Maybe Hackett didn't get everything. There's a jump from the reports about the funeral home, to this stack mentioning Tiffany and Heidi in Scottsdale. It sounds like they were involved in distribution of illegal substances, but the reports that potentially tied them to the funeral home are missing. There must be a connection, but, as of right now, I don't see it."

"I have an idea." Erick grins. "I know that's usually your department, but hear me out."

I flourish my hands in his direction. "Please, enlighten me."

"Maybe I should go back to the fancy hotel and call Delgado. I can tell her about the bullet hole in the door and pretend that you're missing. Maybe she'll give something away."

Chewing the inside of my cheek, I tip my head back and forth like a metronome. "Maybe, but what if she offers to start looking for me? The first thing she would do is put a tail on you. And that would lead them right back to our new hideout."

He wipes some ketchup from his lip. "Our hideout?" Chuckling, he lobs the "plan" volley to me. "Okay, Moon, what's your idea?"

"I say we dangle a carrot. We tell her that we found some new evidence, but because of an attempt on my life, we want to meet in a public place. Then we call her from a series of payphones until we lead her to the final location. That way, we can track her and make sure she's not followed."

"Are there still payphones?" Erick raises an eyebrow.

"Yeah, now that you mention it . . . How about we pick up a third burner phone, and use it for this mission? We lead her on the scavenger hunt, and then we ditch it?"

Erick nods and crosses his arms in a self-satisfied way. "I like it. It gives us the upper hand, and a chance to see if she sells us out."

"Let's finish up with this evidence, in case it disappears, and then head over to see Mr. Hackett in the morning, before we set the wheels in motion with Delgado. Sound good?"

"Sounds about as good as it's gonna get, with a tire-slashing, gun-wielding nut case on our tail."

Muffled shouts from the room on our left and the blaring television from the room on our right fill the void in our conversation while we power through the remaining evidence.

Cold fast-food leftovers serve as our posh dinner.

"And now we should probably address the sleeping situation."

We're both sitting on the lumpy queen-size bed, pawing through papers, and shoving various fried foods in our mouths.

He stretches out on top over the threadbare duvet. "Head to toe? I sleep on top of the covers you sleep underneath?"

Inside, I want to chuckle at his adorable, ten-year-old sleepover rules, but on the outside I play it cool. "Sounds good. But don't kick me in the face."

He sits up. "I would never. Seriously, I'm like a

statue when I sleep. I almost always wake up in the same position as when I went to sleep."

I knit my brow into a very serious sleep researcher expression and push up my imaginary glasses before pretending to write on my invisible clipboard. "Yes, yes, Mr. Harper. Except for when you get up to use the restroom in the middle of the night and get back into the wrong bed. Is that the one exception to your *statue* rule?"

He laughs and reaches across the bed to steal my jalapeño poppers. "You win. Maybe not exactly a statue, but I promise I will not kick you."

Extending my hand I offer a matter-of-fact smile. "Deal."

He grips my hand. "Deal." Without releasing his hold, he pulls me in for a smooch to seal the deal.

Dear Lord baby Jesus! Give me strength! Somehow, I have to focus.

Until bedtime, we turn on the television for background noise as we trade papers back and forth, sharing bits of possibly useful information.

My mood ring flashes with heat and I instantly look toward the television. "Turn it up. Turn it up."

Erick grabs the remote and bumps up the volume.

"A spokesperson for the hotel claims that no one was injured. The alleged bullet hole in the door is under investigation. This is the first attack of this kind to occur in a five-star hotel in the Phoenix Metro area."

He taps the volume back down and his shoulders slump. "So much for our plan to keep that a secret and let them think you were dead."

"Whatever. I got out of there alive, and they don't know where we are. As far as I'm concerned, that's a win for our side. I say we proceed with our plans for tomorrow and see if we can get some information about these Scottsdale chicks from Hackett, or maybe from Delgado. But I don't want to tip our hand."

Erick's mouth is full of fried apple *empanada*, but he nods supportively.

When the harsh morning light blasts through the useless curtains covering our one window, I rub my eyes and look left.

My bunkmate is still sound asleep, and indeed appears to be in the same position as when he lay down.

I check my phone and there's no return call from Silas. Slipping into the bathroom, I splash a little water on my face and exhale.

Erick is still sound asleep when I walk into the main room. I grab a water bottle and rehydrate. As I ease myself down onto my side of the bed, I grab a stack of papers and flip through them halfheartedly while staring unrelentingly at my snoozing guy.

Rather than the warm melty tingles that usually accompany my daydreams, a sharp, icy pain stabs my heart. What if I hadn't been standing beside the door? What if he came back to that hotel room and found me—dead? Do I want to risk loving someone, if they're just going to be taken away? Why should I risk letting someone love me? I don't ever want to cause anyone the kind of pain I had to endure when my mother was taken from me. But maybe that's what love is? Maybe love is something so powerful that it makes you forget the risk.

I stare longingly at Erick's full lips and my tummy finally flip-flops in the good way, and my insides feel warm and tingly.

Maybe it's time to take the risk?

When a loud thud against the left wall of our motel room finally awakens Sheriff Sleepyhead, I'm already dressed and starving for a decent breakfast.

"I finished going through the new evidence while you were having a lie-in." Maybe it's being back in Arizona, maybe it was seeing my old home the other night, or maybe it's reading all these reports about my long-dead mother, but some of her sweet British phrases have been popping to mind unbidden.

He gazes at me and manages a sleepy smile.

"The wig is growing on me." Erick jumps out of bed and stretches himself awake. "Give me two minutes."

I shake my head in disbelief. While I'm well aware that men get ready much faster than women, there's no way he can pull this off in two minutes. When I actually hear him turn on the shower, I roll my eyes. This man is dreaming.

Thirty seconds later, he's out of the bathroom with a low-slung towel around his waist flicking a comb through his hair with one hand, while he brushes his teeth with the other.

Normally, I would be extremely distracted by his exposed torso, but his mind-boggling multi-tasking has my full attention.

He tosses the comb on the counter, rinses his mouth, and scoops up a pile of clothes I hadn't even seen him lay out the night before. He disappears into the bathroom and in less than twenty-five seconds pops back out fully dressed. "Did I make it?"

"Did you make what?"

His shoulders sag and he sighs. "You didn't time me?"

Peals of laughter erupt and I have to hold my stomach as little tears of joy leak out of the corners of my eyes. "No, I wasn't timing you, *Ricky*."

He mopes toward the door. "Come on, Moon. I

saw a greasy spoon around the corner when we were casing this joint."

His use of street-tough vernacular brings a fresh wave of giggles as we load into our minivan. I glance over my shoulder and muse: that's probably the first non-illicit tryst that motel's ever seen!

CHAPTER 17

BREAKFAST IS TOLERABLE, and at least I manage to finish it today.

"Do you need anything from the room, or should we head straight out to see Hackett?"

"Let's head straight out."

On the way, I catch Erick up on the rest of the evidence I plowed through. "So besides the Scottsdale chicks, the other loose end is this Ian Butler. I can't quite piece everything together, because, like I said, there seem to be some reports missing. What exists gives me the feeling that Ian was Hackett's partner, at some point, and had more than a little to do with Hackett's early retirement."

"Any photos of Butler?"

"Nope. You could ask Delgado, but that might raise all kinds of red flags. You know, if she's the one feeding information to some lowlife. We don't want to throw Butler under the bus if he was legitimately trying to solve the case."

Erick nods. "Lemme call Paulsen real quick."

I stare out the window at the Saguaro cactus, which for some reason only grows in Arizona, and try to remember my trip to the Tucson Botanical Gardens with my mother when I was nine. Those memories are in bits and pieces, and my natural snoopiness interferes as I eavesdrop on Erick's conversation.

"So definitely not from smoking. Liquid? We'll check into it. Can I ask one more favor?"

Unconsciously, I lean toward him, expecting an extremely catty response from my least favorite deputy.

Instead, I hear her matter-of-fact Midwestern voice fill in an interesting slice of information.

(Slightly muffled by the phone) "I did a little digging on the Hackett fellow. He ended up in a home because he didn't have any family. Anything else, Sheriff?"

"Actually, I was wondering if you could do a little more digging? On Ian Butler and Vianca Delgado at the Phoenix Metro PD. The usual, you know: commendations, reprimands, that sort of stuff."

I'm fairly certain I hear Deputy Paulsen agree.

"Thanks, Paulsen. Call me when you get something."

He sets his phone in the cup holder in the center console and takes a deep breath.

However, I steal his thunder. "Hackett doesn't have any kids? So who exactly is visiting him every second and fourth Sunday afternoon?"

Erick opens his mouth, closes his mouth, and shakes his head. "So you heard all of that?"

"Well, not the first part. But then I couldn't stop myself from listening in. Sorry."

"Let me summarize. You were right about the nicotine toxicity. Impossible to achieve those levels through smoking. Some type of liquid nicotine would have to have been used. Injection requires a smaller dosage to be fatal, but a larger quantity would be fatal if ingested."

"And, once again, we have no body to exhume and no way to search for an injection site. Based on the toxicology report can we estimate the original dose? Maybe that would help us figure out how it was administered?"

"Most likely. What difference does it make?"

"Probably not that much. But if a hypodermic needle was used, that may lead us in one direction versus another."

He hits his left-hand turn signal and rubs his

lip. "Okay. Let's keep it on the back burner. The bigger issue is this mysterious 'son.' If Hackett doesn't have any next of kin, I think our next priority is finding out who's been visiting him."

"Sure, but you're out of your jurisdiction and I have no relation to the man whatsoever. They're not gonna let us see the visitor logs."

"True. But they can't stop us from running a stakeout on Sunday afternoon."

A broad smile spreads across my face. "We make a good team."

For some reason Erick blushes and becomes obsessed with looking at his side-view mirror.

We pull into the parking lot at Sunny Cactus Retirement Community, and Erick asks me to wait in the car.

"Why?"

"Last time we were here, you caused a real scene. If we come in together, they're likely to suspect it's you—even in the wig. Let me go in and test the waters. You know, see if anyone's noticed anything missing from Hackett's room. I'll signal you if it's all clear."

I'm happy to wait in the car and watch Erick stride toward the entrance in his fabulous jeans.

While I wait, I toy with the idea of calling Silas, but he would definitely see it as an affront if I were to end the call without warning. Less than a minute later Erick is rapidly approaching the minivan.

He gets in, starts the engine, and backs us into a clandestine spot on the other side of a delivery truck.

"Care to share, Sheriff?"

"His 'son' is visiting him right now."

My heart thuds. "What's your next move?"

"We sit tight until we see who walks out of this building. I'll take pictures of everyone who exits and let Paulsen cross reference the images with the names that have popped up in our investigation."

"If they're saying 'son' then it must be a male. That definitely puts Delgado out of the running. I'm not saying she's not feeding some guy information, or working with a male partner, but she's not the one visiting."

"Agreed. On second thought, you better move into the back. I'll run the OP and take the pictures. Two people in a car draws more attention than one. We don't want to blow our cover."

I climb over the center console, slouch low, and cross my arms in a huff in the middle seat.

A young Hispanic couple with a toddler leave about ten minutes later. Erick snaps a picture, even though the nurses clearly didn't mention a family.

About five minutes after that, a young brunette

woman, with two strawberry blonde daughters in tow, heads to their red minivan.

Erick snaps a picture. "This feels a little creepy."

"It's all right. You're not technically a peeping Tom. Your girlfriend is here. So that actually makes us both voyeurs."

He utters a dispirited chuckle. An elderly African-American man with a walker tentatively makes his way down the sidewalk and waits for a taxi to pick him up.

Roughly fifteen minutes later, a tall woman with sunglasses and short red hair, who is anywhere from thirty to fifty years old, strides across the parking lot in a towering pair of heels.

And finally, after a total of forty-five minutes of surveillance, a tall, slope-shouldered Caucasian man, with close-cropped brown hair, strides purposefully toward a Ford Interceptor sedan in the parking lot.

He doesn't exactly squeal the tires as he leaves, but there's a chirp.

"Did you get a picture of him? He looks vaguely familiar . . ."

Erick nods. "That's gotta be our guy. I'm sending the image to Paulsen right now, but I can tell you with one hundred percent certainty that his vehicle was an unmarked squad car."

My ring burns on my left hand and I look down in time to see a used syringe.

I slide the minivan side door open with a crash. "We've got to get in there! Hackett's been poisoned!"

Erick doesn't ask any questions. He jumps out of the vehicle and we run for the front desk.

He skips the niceties, flashes his badge, and commands, "Get a crash cart, emetics, and activated charcoal."

We race down the hallway and find Hackett's door locked. Before an orderly can join us with the key, Erick smashes his shoulder into the door and blasts into the room.

Hackett is convulsing on the bed.

There's no time to be careful or secretive. Taking advantage of the confusion, I bolt forward, slip the amber vial from my pocket, and force the liquid down Hackett's throat.

The doctor and three nurses rush into the room.

Erick pulls me back and I slip the ampoule into my pocket as quickly as possible.

"Mitzy, you shouldn't tamper with a crime scene. What were you doing?"

My head is spinning and I grab the first lie that whirls past. "I thought he was choking. I was trying to clear his airway."

A dark cloud passes through Erick's eyes and he pulls me back against the wall. "Let's step out into the hallway and let these folks do their job."

As I walk to the doorway a weak voice cries out from the bed. "Wait, Miss Moon, wait."

Keith Hackett's feeble plea brings the room to a grinding halt.

The head nurse motions for me to step toward the bed.

"Yes, Mr. Hackett." I grab his outstretched limb with my left hand, and when his fingers touch my mood ring a peaceful calm passes over the body that was so recently writhing in pain.

"Your mother was poisoned. Nicotine. They covered it up. Someone covered it up. I'm sorry."

The effort of such an extended moment of lucidity takes its toll. Mr. Hackett collapses onto his pillow.

I step away from the bed with tears running down my cheeks. Suspicions and theories were one thing; now we have confirmation.

Erick guides me into the hallway and holds me as I process all of the emotions coursing through my veins.

"I need to talk to the director and make sure that guy's visiting privileges are revoked. Permanently. And I think we better run our gambit on

Delgado sooner rather than later. We need to find out who we can trust down here."

Nodding my head, I swipe a thumb under each eye.

Erick's phone pings. He glances down at the text. "It's from Paulsen." He flips the screen toward me. "And Butler's our man."

Staring at the smiling picture of the man we watched race out of the care facility makes my skin crawl. He's a cop, like we thought, and he's suspect number one in this attempt on Hackett's life. "You go talk to the director. I want to make sure Keith is all right."

Erick walks off to take care of logistics and get Butler's visitation revoked, and I lean in the doorway to watch the steady rise and fall of Mr. Hackett's chest.

Did Silas know? Did he have some vision of this future? Or did he honestly give me a universal poison antidote for grins and giggles? That man is a mystery wrapped in an enigma.

Recognizing the regular nurse, I ask her, "Excuse me, is Mr. Hackett going to be all right?"

"He appears to have had a reaction to his morning meds."

Scrunching up my face in disbelief, I pull Mr. Hackett's nurse aside. "Has he ever had a reaction to his meds before?"

"No. Never."

"Did you give him a different medication or different dosage today?"

"No. Same protocol that he's been receiving for the last six months."

The word "ear" echoes through my mind. I glance toward Keith as I continue, "Sheriff Harper is talking to the director right now, but I think you should know, the man who's been visiting him isn't his son."

Her whole body stiffens and her pupils dilate. "I knew it. I knew something wasn't right. Every time that man visited, Mr. Hackett had a bout of *mal de ojo*."

"I'm not familiar with that term."

"My *abuela*, my grandmother, was a *curandera*. She used to say that some people have a dark energy. And the poison in their energy seeps into the weak. I think Mr. Hackett was susceptible to that man's evil energy."

I've never met anyone who speaks so openly about the energetic realm, outside of those paid to do so in boutiques in Sedona. "That could definitely have something to do with it. Anyway, I thought you should know— Is that blood?" I point to a trickle behind Keith's right ear.

She nods and performs the sign of the cross before hurrying to Mr. Hackett's side. She wipes away the trickle of blood with a sterile alcohol pad and gasps.

"What is it?" I move to her side.

"A small puncture wound." She hits the red emergency button. "It could be from a hypodermic needle."

CHAPTER 18

TIME TO DANGLE the carrot in front of Detective Delgado and see if she bites. Using our third burner phone to lay the trail of breadcrumbs, Erick and I begin *The Most Dangerous Game*.

"Detective Delgado? Hi, it's Mitzy Moon. I have some new information about my mother's case and I was wondering if you could meet me?"

Erick pulls the minivan over, taps some information into his phone, and shows me an address.

"Great. I'll text you the address."

I end the call and flash my eyebrows. "She's on the hook."

He drives to the first location, while I text her the address and a time. The idea is to get there first and scope out the surrounding area. We have to verify that she arrives at the first spot alone before we send her to the next location.

As the clock ticks down to the time of our first meeting we both see the shoulder-length dark hair and confident stride of Detective Delgado at the same time.

She's seven minutes early.

Erick methodically scans the surrounding area. "Looks like she's alone."

I grab the phone, but he puts a firm hand on mine. "Wait. If you enter the next location the second she walks into this one, she'll know we're watching her. Wait until a minute past the time of the meeting, and then send the next location. She's a smart detective. I'm sure she knows what we're doing, but let's string her out as long as we can."

Nodding my head in admiration, I have to acknowledge this isn't his first *rodeo*. Sheriff Harper is a seasoned law-enforcement professional and my extrasensory perceptions may allow me to stay one step ahead of him, but that's more luck than skill. I can probably learn a thing or two, if I can swallow my pride for a couple of minutes.

"Okay, Moon. Enter the next location."

"Copy that."

Cut to— the third location in our scavenger hunt and we still haven't seen anyone following the detective.

"What do you think? Should we make the next location the last one?" Erick leans toward me expectantly.

"Yeah. I don't think she's being followed."

We send the last location and time, and race to get there before her. We've chosen a very small *taquería*, with nothing but parking lot surrounding it. We can easily see any other vehicles in the area, and there's no tree line, or balcony that could hide a sniper.

"Do we wait inside? Or do we wait here?" I tap my fingers anxiously on the dash.

Erick smiles. "We wait here. We want to make absolutely sure she's not followed." He scans the horizon, searching for her vehicle.

"And her gun?"

He looks at me. "What about it?"

"If she takes her gun inside, we wouldn't be able to see if she draws her weapon before we enter."

"She's here." Erick locks onto the vehicle and watches the detective back strategically into a parking spot. "Mitzy, text this, exactly: 'Step out of the vehicle, remove your weapon, and place it on the dashboard before you come inside."

My little texting thumbs are tapping as fast as they can.

Delgado steps out of the vehicle and looks toward the small taco stand. She pulls out her weapon, hooks the trigger guard over the pointer finger of her right hand, and holds it up in plain sight. She then slides it onto the dash of her vehicle and closes the driver-side door. She walks toward the little restaurant unarmed and without hesitation.

Erick grumbles something under his breath.

"What did you say?"

"Nothing. She's awfully confident for someone working alone."

"You think there's someone tailing her that we didn't see?"

He shrugs. "Let's enter through the back door."

We exit the minivan and approach the warped screen door banging in the desert breeze at the back of the *taquería*.

He opens the door and brandishes his badge, while I hold a finger over my lips.

The employees are fearful, but extremely cooperative, and after we pass through the cramped kitchen into the tiny seating area, we're able to confirm that Delgado is alone.

Erick puts away his badge, sits down next to her, and pulls his gun.

I take the seat opposite.

"Whatever you two have must be pretty important to take me on a wild-goose chase like that." She nods in my direction. "Nice wig."

To her credit, Delgado isn't nervous. And I'm using all of my regular and psychic senses to confirm that. "It's starting to look like my mom was murdered by a dirty cop. I know you said you weren't on the force back then, but maybe you're working with the person who was."

Delgado shakes her head, and her dark-brown eyes do not hesitate to look deeply into mine. "Look, Moon, I don't know what the two of you uncovered, but I can guarantee you that I would never tarnish the shield." Her jaw clenches and I feel her anger at the accusation swell. "I'm clean, and I can help you."

I swallow hard and look at Erick. All my senses are telling me that she's the real deal. Everything she said rings true, but I need some indication from him that he feels the same.

He holsters his gun, exhales, and leans back. "It's good to hear you say that, Delgado. We really need someone on our side."

Sensing the drop in tension, a young server approaches the table.

Without waiting for our input, Detective Delgado places our order in Spanish.

As the server walks away, I nod my head. "I definitely got *pollo* and *papas fritas*."

The hard lines of her face soften and she smiles. "I don't think you'll be disappointed. This is actually one of the best *taquerías* on this side of town."

"I guess that's what happens when you use online star-ratings to select your clandestine locations." I shrug and return her grin.

A round of laughter passes over the table, and I genuinely feel that I can trust Delgado.

She looks meaningfully from me to Erick and back. "You mentioned a dirty cop. What evidence do you have?"

He holds up a hand, and I have to bite my tongue as I let him take the lead.

"There's a cop whose name appears on the cremation orders for Mitzy's mother's remains. That same officer has been posing as Mr. Hackett's son for the last six months. Today, there was an attempt on Mr. Hackett's life and this officer was witnessed fleeing the scene."

Delgado's shoulders slump. "You got a name?"

Erick glances around the tiny space to make sure he won't be overheard. "Ian Butler."

A strange series of emotions swirl through the detective. At first my clairsentience picks up on a strong vibe of disbelief. But as the seconds tick past, I can feel her weighing the information and eventually accepting it, and possibly even believing it to be true.

"I have to say, I'm surprised and not surprised at

the same time. Butler's been involved in a lot of undercover operations. Some questionable things have happened, but I never believed the rumors. This kinda sheds new light on things."

The food arrives and the spicy aromas bring instant growls to my stomach. "This looks delicious."

Delgado smiles. "Yeah, I keep telling them to expand. Who needs such a big parking lot when the place seats twenty people? But he likes to leave it small and keep the quality high."

Erick barely swallows his food before he chimes in. "This guy knows exactly what he's doing. Never question a man with this much skill in the kitchen."

I tilt my head. "Duly noted."

The next few minutes are occupied with serious eating. The chicken is cooked to perfection and the *pico de gallo* has the exact right amount of cilantro. I had almost forgotten the joys of Mexican food in the Southwest.

Erick smiles across the table. "Looks like you're enjoying your culinary tour of Arizona, Moon."

Before I can reply, Delgado pipes up. "So what's the deal with you two? I don't know a lot of sheriffs that would travel halfway across the country to work on a cold case—for a friend."

I busy myself with blushing, while Erick responds. "I'd say our friendship might have gotten off to a rocky start, but in the end we had more in common than we thought."

Covering my mouth to prevent losing any bits of *papas fritas*, I have to share my side. "Rocky start? He tried to arrest me for the murder of my own grandfather!"

Delgado smiles and amusement sparkles in her eyes. "So you're battle buddies. That's a bond that lasts for life."

Erick wipes his mouth with a napkin and turns toward the detective. "Did you serve?"

"Marine Corps Reserve, eight years. I saw some action in Kandahar. You?"

"Army. Two tours. Afghanistan."

Something unspoken passes between them, and the feelings of trust grow. I think Delgado can really help us. I hope I'm not wrong.

We finished our lunch and the detective promises to dig into Ian Butler when she gets back to the precinct. She warns us not to share the information with anyone else and to keep using burner phones.

Back at our shady motel, Erick suggests a snack and water run.

"Yeah, go ahead. I'll hang out here, if that's cool

with you. I need to call home and make sure every-one's all right."

He nods and pauses with one hand on the door-knob. "And by 'everyone' you mean your one cat with two names?"

Ignoring his jab, I take another tack. "Yes, and Twiggy, and Silas. And I might even ask about Odell."

He grins. "Impressive list. I'll be back as quick as I can. Don't answer calls from any number you don't recognize. I'll pick up a new burner phone too."

Despite the feelings of trust that we exchanged with Detective Delgado, Erick is still considering ditching the burner phone we used to lure her to the meeting. Just in case.

As soon as he leaves, I dial the bookshop back in Pin Cherry Harbor.

"Mitzy!" Ghost-ma swirls anxiously in front of the Phoom camera.

"Hi, Grams. What's up? Why are you so agitated?"

The large grey mustache and wagging jowls of my alchemist/attorney dip into frame. "Is that you, Mizithra? What kind of a hovel are you occupying? I am certain your inheritance could provide for more satisfactory accommodation."

The warmth of family love fills my heart.

"We're on the run, Silas. Some shenanigans went down and Erick and I thought it would be best if we ditched our phones—"

"That's what happened!" Grams is clutching her pearls and sighing dramatically. "Pyewacket and I called several times and it kept telling us that Mitzy Moon was unavailable."

Remembering my duties as an afterlife interpreter, I bring Silas up to speed on Ghost-ma's comments while he slips the wire arms of his bespelled spectacles behind his large ears. Now he can see Grams as I share her words.

"It was wise of you to take precautions. Is Sheriff Harper's room near yours? I assume he arranged it so that he would be able to protect you."

I twist uncomfortably on the bed and avoid answering the question. "Hey, did you have some kind of a premonition?"

Grams and Silas reply in unison. "Who? Me?"

The fact that their responses are so perfectly timed even though Silas can't hear her sends me into a fit of giggles.

"Take a deep breath, Mizithra. Were you speaking to me or your grandmother?"

"I was actually talking to you, Silas. I had to use that anti-poison that you gave me."

Grams pushes through Silas and he shivers with

a bad case of ghost-chills before stepping away from the camera.

The shimmering, panicked image of my ghostly grandmother nearly swallows the lens. "What? You need to come home. Solving this case is not worth losing your life, dear."

"Reow." Can confirm.

"It wasn't me." I go on to explain the whole story of my vision and the attempt to poison Mr. Hackett. I thank Silas for providing the amber vial of liquid that ultimately saved Mr. Hackett's life.

Rather than cheers, applause, or additional questions, Silas drops into the chair, smooths his mustache with a thumb and forefinger and nods. "That explains a great deal."

Silence.

"Well, I'm glad it explains something to you, because all it did for me was raise more questions. What are you talking about?"

Silas leans too close to the camera, and all I can see are jowls and a bit of ear hair. "Silas, you have to sit back. You're way too close to the camera." I look away and mumble, "Way too close."

"Robin Pyewacket Goodfellow was acting very ill this morning. In fact, Twiggy called and requested I come and have a look at him, to assist in determining if a trip to the vet was in order."

"The vet? What's wrong with Mr. Cuddlekins?"

"As it turns out, nothing. But he must've had some premonition of his own regarding the poisoning. When I arrived he was lethargic and one of his legs was twitching. I looked him over and he appeared to be unharmed, physically. Within a few moments of my examination his behavior returned to normal and he consumed two bowls of Fruity Puffs."

"About what time was that?"

"A little more than two hours ago."

"Pye, someday you'll have to tell me how you do it."

"Ree-ow." Soft but condescending.

Shaking my head, I ignore the pompous feline. "That's almost the exact time I discovered Mr. Hackett convulsing and administered the antidote."

Silas steeples his fingers and bounces his chin on his pointers. "A truly remarkable species."

Grams swoops in and her ethereal fingers scratch between Pye's black-tufted ears. "What are you wearing, sweetie?"

"Seriously, Grams? I tell you about an attempt on my life and saving a victim of poisoning, and your first question is what am I wearing?"

Silas chuckles at my response.

Grams abandons Pyewacket and her image freeze frames and flickers.

"Grams? What is it? What happened?"

"Attempt on your life? Attempt on your life! Mizithra Achelois Moon, you get your ample behind on a plane this instant. You are done playing Wild West vigilante." Sparkling tears trickle down her cheeks. "I'm not going to lose you after I just found you."

I attempt to ignore her ghost-rant. "Silas, are you sure you don't know some magic—hold on, let me correct that—alchemical transmutation to give her an afterlife handkerchief?"

We all share a round of laughter. "I assume Isadora's tears are in response to the threats on your life. How are you keeping yourself safe?"

"Erick and I are using burner phones and we've relocated to this less-than-desirable motel to keep off the radar. We're paying for everything in cash. Tilly made some transfers at the bank. Initially we were trying to play it like I was dead, but the previous hotel held a press conference claiming no one was injured, so that ruined our whole plan."

Grams springs to life. "Being alive ruined your plan. What on earth is going on down there? I don't like this investigation one bit. You're down there without backup, you probably don't even have a murder wall . . . I can't imagine how you're surviving."

I share her concerns with Silas.

"I do hope you are using the utmost caution, Mitzy. Do you have any solid leads?"

"Unfortunately, yes. And the reason I say unfortunately is because our most solid lead points to a dirty cop. We think we have someone on the inside we can trust, but it probably is a little more dangerous than I'd hoped."

Grams gasps and disapparates.

Silas leans forward in concern, but with his bulbous nose that close to a fisheye lens, the gesture brings a fresh set of giggles.

"You have to lean back." I smile happily at my mentor and my sweet fur baby.

Grams pops back in and she seems to have calmed herself. Her energy is more stable. "You never did answer the question."

"Which question?"

"The one about Erick's room—"

As luck would have it, at that exact moment the door to *our* room opens. Erick pops in and starts talking. "So I grabbed us some savory snacks, some sweet snacks, a couple of pops, a bottle of wine, and two waters. That should get us through a little more research and maybe a late night movie. Did I forget anything?"

Silas puts a hand over his mouth to hide his grin, while Grams attacks.

"Us? Late night movie? Are you sharing a—"

TAP.

I end the call and attempt a nonchalant pose as Erick drops his grocery bags on the floor and sizes me up.

"Who were you talking to?"

"Silas. And my cat."

"Then why do you look so guilty? I already know all about your secret friendship with the four-leggeds."

"Ha ha. Mind your own business." I lay my phone next to the "No Smoking" ashtray and clap my hands in anticipation. "Now let's get into this research and, more importantly, these snacks."

He retrieves the two bags from the floor, holds them toward me as a peace offering, and asks, "Is there room for two on there?"

Oh brother. This is going to be a long night.

CHAPTER 19

THE UNRELENTING DESERT sun blasts into our fleabag motel. I blink my eyes against the harsh light, and I move to wipe the drool from the corner of my mouth. En route, I become aware of an arm encircling me—an arm that is not my own.

My heart thuds in my chest, and the heat of Erick's slow, steady breathing on the back of my head makes my skin tingle. I don't even remember falling asleep. But somewhere between finishing the bottle of wine and my second bag of pretzels, I definitely did drift off to dreamland.

The problem is, I can't be sure that I'm not still there. Waking up as a "little spoon" with Erick's arm draped over me is definitely one of my recurring fantasies.

Best give myself a little pinch, lest I fall into the trap of believing this daydream is reality.

I slide my fingers over and pinch my own arm skin.

Suppressing a yelp, I'm forced to admit I'm awake.

Rather than risk spoiling this perfect moment with discovery, it's best if I slip away and hope he wakes up while I'm in the bathroom.

However, his arm is quite a bit heavier than I might've assumed. The idea of lifting it effortlessly and slipping away without waking him, like every rom-com movie I've ever seen, is becoming a difficult proposal.

I've only half-escaped when Erick stirs and re-secures his grip.

Although, now that I've adjusted my position, his hand has fallen into a rather inconvenient region of my torso. As I attempt to get his hand off my upper chest . . . sleeping handsome awakes.

Our nearness definitely shocks him and his muscle spasm delivers a most unwelcome squeeze.

"Ouch."

He sits bolt upright and rubs a hand over his face. "I'm so sorry. I didn't mean to— That was completely out of— Are you all right?"

Crossing my arms over my injured boob area, I

giggle helplessly. "I'm fine. And for future reference, I'm not into that sort of thing."

He blushes a terrific shade of magenta and
laughs as he collapses back onto the bed. "It really
was an accident, Moon. I'm definitely sorry."

I jump up and manically collect papers from
my side of the bed. "The thing that caught my eye
before I drifted off was that Hackett's original
partner was killed in action. The timeline's a little
fuzzy, but it seems like he worked without a partner
for a few years, until Ian Butler was assigned to
work with him. Should we ask Delgado to look into
what happened to Hackett's previous partner?"

Erick rubs the sleep from his eyes. "I say we put
the analysis of evidence on the back burner until
after breakfast. I got two or three hours sleep, and
now you're asking me to engage my brain's full capacity without benefit of coffee. Not sure I can
deliver."

"Copy that." I drop the rest of the files into the
box, secure the lid, and exhale. "I think my brain got
an extra boost from the rush of pinch-induced
adrenaline. But I could definitely use some black
gold myself. You want to head back over to that
taquería for some breakfast burritos?"

"That sounds divine." He winks.

"You're a regular standup comic, Sheriff." I
shake my head at his mockery of my tendency to

use the word "divine" under pressure. "Give me five minutes, and I'll be ready to head out."

Erick grabs his phone swipes, taps, and shouts, "Go! Clock's ticking."

Giggling, I shake my head and make half an attempt to run to the bathroom.

As we start to pull into the little taco restaurant parking lot, Erick suddenly jerks the wheel back onto the road and continues straight.

"What? That's the place."

"Yeah, I know. But I saw Delgado's car in the parking lot."

"That's all right. We know she's familiar with the place. She's on our side, right?"

"Maybe, but that unmarked car we saw legging it out of the retirement community was parked right next to hers."

"What? Ian Butler is meeting her for breakfast? That's pretty sketchy. I felt like I could really trust her."

"Yeah, me too. Looks like it's greasy drive-through for us this morning."

I pretend to slump my shoulders in disappointment, but I seriously have no problem with eggy muffins and delicious hash brown patties.

Halfway through a stack of pancakes that Odell

certainly would've scraped into the trash, Erick's phone rings.

"It's Delgado. Should I answer?"

I nod my head furiously. "Yes! Answer. As far as she knows we still think she's on our side. Answer the call and play dumb, if that's possible."

He shoves a plastic spork-full of pancakes in his mouth and I wrinkle my brow in confusion.

Erick grabs his phone and answers without swallowing. "Sheriff Harper. Sorry, force of habit. Oh, we're finishing up breakfast." He swallows his food. "You? With Butler?" He looks at me and smiles.

The word "safe" pops into my head and I nod a silent thanks to my claircognizance.

He finishes the call and brings me up to speed. "That was Delgado, obviously. She called to say she had breakfast with Butler—"

"So she wasn't trying to do something behind our backs?"

He smiles patiently. "As I was saying. She had breakfast with Butler to try to build some rapport. He's kind of a lone wolf in the department and she didn't want to start questioning him about your mom's case without laying some groundwork. Unfortunately, he got called away before she could set up another meeting."

"Anything else?"

"She did some digging and matched the Tiffany mentioned in some of the CI reports with a witness statement in a domestic disturbance. Delgado says she's a soccer mom living in a gated community in Scottsdale. She wasn't able to draw any connection to the case your mother was working with Butler, though."

My mood ring is a fiery circle on my left hand and I can't ignore it any longer. I glance down and see two women kicking a soccer ball back and forth. "There's got to be more to this Tiffany lead. Her name's coming up too often. Did Delgado say if Heidi lives in the same gated community as Tiffany?"

He calls the detective without hesitation. His belief in my hunches is bordering on astonishing.

"Yeah, it's Harper. Were there any other residents of that gated community mentioned in the information you uncovered? Maybe a 'Heidi'? Really? No sign of her? That is strange. I'll let Mitzy know. Thanks."

"What did she say?"

"She said about a decade ago there was a disturbance call to the residence of Heidi Faulk, who lived across the cul-de-sac from Tiffany. According to all the neighbors' statements Heidi and her husband had a falling out and she went to visit a sister in Australia."

"Australia? Who has a sister in Australia?"

Erick scrunches up his face and shrugs. "I would imagine people from Australia."

"Fair point. So she heads off to visit a sister in Australia ten years ago and no one wonders why she didn't come back?"

"Delgado didn't say she didn't come back. Those were statements from a decade ago. Once the case was closed, no one followed up. She could be sitting in that house right now. We can go check it out if you want? Delgado's texting me the information about this exclusive housing development in Scottsdale."

I wiggle my shoulders. "This sounds like a perfect opportunity to wear something else from my giant suitcase."

He raises his hands and waves them in the air. "Hallelujah."

We drive the short distance back to the motel. As we pull up, the door of our room stands open and a maid's cart is parked outside.

Erick jumps out of the minivan and charges toward the room.

I manage to intercept him. "Slow down. Slow down. Let me handle it. You back me up."

His hand is already on the grip of the gun tucked at his back in a decidedly "Paulsen-esque" maneuver. "Okay. I'll cover you."

I step into the room and the maid doesn't turn. She's tucking fresh sheets onto the bed.

"Excuse me. Excuse me."

She still doesn't turn, but that's when I notice the thin cords from her ears to her phone. I step forward, tap her on the shoulder and jump back in case she comes out swinging.

She turns around in shock and rips the earbuds from her ears. "Disculpe."

Smiling warmly, I attempt to relieve her of her duties in our room. "You don't need to clean. We don't need cleaning." I wave my hands around the room like an idiot.

She shakes her head. "No hablo inglés."

The good news is, if she doesn't speak English, she probably doesn't read English. So the chances of her seeing any sensitive information are rather slim. I take a deep breath and reach out with my extra senses. "You really don't speak any English?"

Her eyes stare at me with concern, but she repeats her earlier reply. "No hablo inglés."

All my senses, regular and extra, confirm that she's telling the truth. I grab my phone and quickly translate a phrase. "No necesitamos que limpies nuestra habitación. No hay limpieza nunca." Between my questionable pronunciation and the inevitable errors of online translators, all I can do is cross my fingers.

She nods. "Si. Si." She leaves the room immediately, but jumps a little when she sees Erick lurking outside the door.

He comes in and quickly closes the door. "How do you know she was telling the truth? What if she does speak English and she was purposely looking through the files? Maybe we should relocate again."

"No. She was telling the truth. And the box is undisturbed. Trust me, all right?"

He sighs and takes his hand off his gun. "Okay. You get changed and I'll put the evidence in the van. I think we've gotten everything we can from these old reports. We need to uncover some fresh evidence. There's no chance of finding a killer if all we have are tracks that ran cold ten years ago."

"Copy that."

I flop my massive suitcase open on the bed and select a designer sundress and the highest heels that I allowed Grams to pack. I begin the process of putting on my face before I fiddle with wig placement.

Once my sophisticated makeup is finished and my messy, wavy *ombré* locks are bobby-pinned into place, I hop into the bathroom and change into my fancy digs.

As I walk out, Erick whistles. "I feel underdressed, Moon. Should I spruce myself up so I can keep pace?"

Blushing, I look down at the floor. "I'm never going to say no to seeing you spruced up."

He steps closer. "That almost sounded like a compliment."

I playfully punch him on the arm. "You have five minutes." I grab my phone and hit the stopwatch. "Clock's ticking."

CHAPTER 20

THE TRUE SOUL of Scottsdale is not for the faint of heart. Imagine Beverly Hills, but instead of manicured lawns there are carefully curated cactus ensembles, rock gardens, and sculpture accents. The backyards do contain swimming pools, but most have extensive patios that provide shade and automatic misters to spritz the nipped and tucked guests with a fine spray of cool water, which evaporates as soon as it touches the skin. This is the *Silicone* Valley.

At the entrance to the gated community, Riparian Knolls, Erick shows his badge and mentions Detective Delgado. Unlike our previous interactions with civilians, this gate attendant is thoroughly unimpressed.

"Sit tight. I'll have to make a call."

Erick glances at me with surprise and a small amount of admiration brightening his features.

The power-mad attendant returns. "This Detective Delgado said you don't have a warrant. But she did request our cooperation. I can officially give you thirty minutes inside the compound. Please check out with me at the gate when you leave. And if there's any report of trouble I'll have you forcibly removed."

He taps his hand on the driver's side door, returns to his air-conditioned booth, and the ornate metal gate rolls open.

As soon as the window goes up, I blurt, "Does Paulsen have a long-lost brother you don't know about?"

Erick drives onward and chuckles under his breath. "I hope nobody ever gives that guy a badge, or a gun. He's on a serious power trip with nothing more than a button that controls a gate arm."

"Right? He takes his job way, way too seriously."

Tapping his thumb on the steering wheel, Erick looks for the address.

A positive flip side pops into my head. "Although, it definitely means that random strangers aren't wandering in and out of this community."

The hairs on the back of my neck tingle, but I'm not sure why.

We make a left turn at Twist Flower Road and a right onto Snapdragon Lane, which becomes Snapdragon Circle.

Erick parks half a block shy of the cul-de-sac. "If this place is as tight as it seems, there are probably already two or three people looking out their windows activating the phone tree."

His comment catches me off guard and I have to laugh before I reply. "This definitely looks like the kind of neighborhood with more than one Gladys Kravitz."

Sadly he doesn't get my *Bewitched* reference, but he gives me a courtesy laugh. "So, do you want to go talk to Tiffany and I'll see who's manning the door at Heidi's old place? Or vice versa?"

Before I answer, I have to weigh the odds. I'd prefer to do both, so that my psychic senses would have the advantage of picking up a reading from Tiffany and gathering whatever details are to be had regarding the possibly missing Heidi. However, at this point I think I'd rather deal with the "one in the hand" than whatever's possibly hiding in the hedges, or whatever that saying is. "I'll take Tiffany, Sheriff."

He puts a hand on his door and turns back. "I'd wish you luck, but it seems like you make your own."

When we exit the vehicle, the wall of heat hits

me like a pizza oven. The dry fiery air seems impossible to inhale. I can feel the heat radiating up through the soles of my designer heels. For the first time in my life I actually wish I were wearing a higher, platform shoe. I might spontaneously combust before I ever reach Tiffany's door.

Taking a deep breath, I prepare to spin my tale. I ring the doorbell and a voice comes over the intercom.

"Thanks. But we don't need any. Please leave or I'll have to call security."

I smile into the doorbell camera and wave. "I'm so sorry to bother you. I was looking at the home over on Twist Flower and was hoping someone could give me a little background about the neighborhood." Thank goodness I saw that "For Sale" sign! Hopefully she'll buy what I'm selling, now.

"The Tuscan two-story?"

"No, it's the three-story with the four-car garage."

"What did you say your name was?"

Ruh-roh, Shaggy, I forgot to prepare an identity. I guess I'll have to grab the first two names that come to mind. "Oh, I didn't, darling. But it's Isadora Harper." Forgive me, Grams and Erick. I didn't have much time.

The front door opens, and the crease-free, peaches-and-cream complexion of the utterly ageless Tiffany stares at me with lingering doubts. "You may as well step into the foyer. But I warn you, I have the security guard on speed dial."

"Thank you. And that's smart. I'd do the same."

She closes the door behind me and not so subtly evaluates my dress and shoes.

My extrasensory data confirms that she is duly impressed.

She begins her interrogation. "Is that a Veronica Beard?"

I silently thank Grams for her unrequested fashion lessons. "It's Carolina Herrera. She has a better line for my body type."

Tiffany nods and tilts her head. "Do you have children?"

"Not yet. My husband and I wanted a few years on our own before we added that complication."

Tiffany nods and clicks her manicured gel nails. "That's wise. I started too young, and it definitely cramped my style."

Attempting a sympathetic nod, I ask, "Have you lived in the community long?"

I sense her struggling with her answer. But there's a small part of me that suddenly realizes it's not that she's hesitant to answer my question, per se; she doesn't want to give her age away.

"I suppose it's been ten or fifteen years. Who can remember? Time flies."

"Oh, of course. Do you know any of your neighbors?"

"Absolutely. All of them. You can't be too careful. You know what I mean?"

Her words continue to have a superficial sweetness, but I'm picking up a sour undercurrent. My mood ring burns with information, but I can't risk a glance. "Do people come and go often, or is it a fairly stable neighborhood?"

Her heart rate increases. "It's a very exclusive community. Once people get in, they rarely leave."

"That's reassuring. What about divorce? It seems so difficult to maintain a healthy marriage if everyone's falling apart around you. Any of your neighbors divorced?"

Her heart rate briefly speeds up, and then takes a striking turn. Her jaw tightens and I feel that if she could scowl, she would. "Gossip is an ugly habit."

I widen my eyes and hope that I'm exuding innocence. "I'm so sorry. You misunderstand. I haven't been married long and . . . not to sound like 'that girl,' but my husband is really good looking. I want to make sure we're in a neighborhood of happily married women. If you know what I mean?"

Her eyes dart toward the door, and if I draw an imaginary line between that gaze and the other homes in the cul-de-sac, I'd say it's a direct hit for Heidi Faulk's house.

"Everyone around here is happily married, as far as I know. As I mentioned, I'm not one to gossip."

"Of course. Well, I appreciate all the information and I hope we get to be neighbors . . ." I extend my hand and wait for a name.

There's a knock on the door and Tiffany stiffens. Her gaze darts toward a drawer in the hallway table. I don't need psychic senses to know what's in that drawer.

"I should probably get going." Turning, I open the door and I'm unsurprised to see Erick on the other side. Time for me to leap into my cover before he blows it. "Sweetie, I told you I'd meet you back at the car." Turning to Tiffany, I add, "This is my husband. Erick. This lovely lady might be our new neighbor if we make an offer on that house on Twist Flower." Wink.

Erick reaches a hand toward Tiffany and offers one of his knee-weakening smiles.

Its power is not lost on the socialite. She smiles as best she can beneath the Botox, and rifles an eager hand toward Erick's. "Very nice to meet you, Mr. Harper. I'm Tiffany. Your wife is quite sweet. We'll have to have you over for cocktails once you get settled into your new place."

I'm struggling not to throw a right hook at this drooling seductress. If there was any doubt in my mind about her cross-cul-de-sac indiscretions, that doubt has vanished. "We better be going, sweetie. We have so many other places to see."

Tiffany tightens her grip on Erick's hand. "I certainly hope Riparian Knolls is at the top of your list."

Erick gifts her with another grin and nods. "Me too."

We hurry back to the minivan and, despite throwing the air conditioning on its highest setting, there is little relief inside the hotbox.

"What was all that smiling and flirting, Sheriff?" My voice is laced with jealousy.

Erick makes a U-turn on the street, to avoid driving in front of Tiffany's house, and heads for the gate. "I was struggling to play the hand you dealt me, Moon. I had no idea I was opening that door to discover my wife." He chuckles.

"Well Tiffany is a lecherous shrew, and she absolutely had or is still having an affair with Heidi's husband?" My arms are crossed and my bottom lip may be having a little pout. "Would it be so bad to have a wife like me?"

His face blushes with a hint of pink. "A wife *like* you, or you for a wife?"

Now it's my turn to squirm with discomfort.

"Never mind. What about Tiffany and the affair with Heidi's husband."

"I'd say it's still going on. A maid answered the door at the Faulk residence. Once I flashed my badge she spilled her guts. Heidi did not return home from Australia. And the woman also claimed no letters or postcards have arrived from overseas. She mentioned a lot of special visits from concerned neighbors, but none more than Tiffany."

He stops the minivan at the exit.

The gate-fascist approaches the vehicle and signals for Erick to put down his window. "That was a one-time thing," he warns.

Erick nods. "Thanks for your cooperation."

The man scowls and returns to his posh booth. The large iron gate rolls back, at a snail's pace, and we leave the community.

"Something's definitely going on with Tiffany. She keeps a gun in the drawer of her hall table and she got real skittish when I asked about her neighbors."

"Maybe you can try to find this missing Heidi."

I tilt my head. "What do you mean?"

"Sometimes you seem to get hunches about where people might be. I don't know how you do it, and it's not like you're sharing the details, but maybe you can get a *hunch* about Heidi."

My thoughts go to the pendulum in my backpack and I wonder if I have the courage to use it in front of Erick? Maybe I can send him on some kind of errand. Plus, I only know how to use it with a map of the area I intend to search. If she could be anywhere in the world, how can I possibly get a map that big? "Maybe."

Erick suggests a fancy lunch since we're already dressed up, but my stomach is churning with too many questions.

"Actually, I was hoping you could drop me off at the motel and grab takeout from somewhere. I kind of have a lot on my mind right now."

He nods. "Of course. Whatever you need."

We swing by the motel, he sees me safely into the room, and promises to return with something amazing.

As soon as he leaves I call Silas. "Good afternoon, Mr. Willoughby. I've run into some trouble and I'm hoping you have a solution."

Never one to cut corners, Silas returns my pleasantries and brings me up to speed on the happenings in Pin Cherry Harbor. This of course takes less than fifteen seconds, since there really isn't anything happening in Pin Cherry. Once we've laid all of that to rest, he's willing to hear my request.

"I need to locate someone. I have the pendulum, and I understand that I have to be very specific with my question. The problem is, she could be anywhere in the world."

He mentions that anyone could be anywhere in the world, but using something called Occam's razor he instructs me to begin with the simplest solution.

"Well, the simplest solution would be that she never left Scottsdale."

He wholeheartedly agrees with me.

"So are you saying she maybe bought herself a new identity? Maybe she's right here under their noses?"

He indicates that a number of options are at play, but that my best bet would be to start with a map of the local area and expand my search if necessary.

"Thanks, Silas. I do always appreciate your calm, rational advice."

Ending the call, I dial Erick to add a quick item to his food run.

To his credit, he doesn't ask me a bunch of questions about why I need a map of the Phoenix Metro area as well as a map of Arizona, he simply agrees to get them for me.

I'm starting to think this man is an angel fallen straight from heaven.

CHAPTER 21

RIGHT ABOUT THE time I start to worry, my knight
in perfect blue jeans returns. In case you're not familiar, let me describe perfect. Did you watch the
very first *Thor*, starring Chris Hemsworth? If not,
my heart goes out to you. If so, think back to the
scene where he's shirtless, and the camera's pushing
in from behind. The way those dungarees rest low
on his hips, not gangster low, just sexy-man low;
those are the perfect jeans.

My apologies for the denim exposition, but if I
didn't clear that dungaree-related preoccupation
out of my head I might not be able to focus for this
next part of the evening.

Erick tosses three maps onto the bed and sets
the bag of take-out on the nightstand. "How do you
feel about pulled-pork tacos, fresh-made tortilla

chips, reportedly 'very hot' salsa, and homemade apple *empanadas* for dessert?"

My whole face lights up. "I feel extremely positive." Pushing the maps aside, I take a seat on the bed and try to arrange the takeout boxes in a user-friendly pattern.

He sits down on the opposite side of the chips and salsa station and hands me two napkins.

"These chips are amazing," I mumble with my mouth full.

Erick shoves a dangerously overloaded tortilla chip into his mouth and his eyes water from the heat. "And the salsa is—as advertised." He grabs his soda and sucks down almost half.

"Easy, Sheriff. You don't want to run out of soda before we destroy these chips."

In the end, our late-afternoon meal disappears without a trace.

"Why don't I get rid of this trash, while you—"

I swallow and try to keep my answer vague. "I'll look at the maps."

He collects all of the trash as I open up the three maps. Using the suggestion from Silas, I start with the Phoenix Metro map. Unzipping the side pocket of my rucksack, I pull out the pendulum and hold it self-consciously in my hand.

Erick ties off the sack of empty take-out containers and leans it against the door. "Whatcha got there?"

Several answers fight for attention. However, it doesn't feel right to "out" Silas without asking his permission. I hate to be dishonest with Erick, but, when in doubt, lie it out. "You're going to think it's really stupid and possibly crazy, but it's something I learned in Sedona from this chick named Galaxie Wonder." The name is that of an actual tarot card reader who kept a stack of business cards in one of the coffee shops where I once worked.

He crosses his arms over his chest. "That's some name. This I gotta see."

"You don't *have* to see. You could take that stuff out to the waste bin and maybe go for a little walk." I nod my head encouragingly.

He drops cross-legged onto the floor. "No. I'm good."

Gulp. It feels like my Adam's apple is twice as large as normal. Wait, do I have an Adam's apple? Maybe only "Adams" have Adam's apples. I suppose I'm technically an Eve. Stop stalling. You're going to have to perform this magic trick in front of him at some point. Making a silent apology to Silas for calling it magic, I smooth the map and wiggle the pendulum to let the chain straighten itself.

"What is that thing?" He leans forward.

"Look, Sheriff, you're welcome to stay, but

you're gonna have to be quiet. I know it sounds weird, but I really have to focus."

He puts his hands up in surrender and presses his full, pouty lips together.

He can't possibly know how distracting that is.

Shaking my head, I close my eyes and take three deep cleansing breaths. I'm sure there's a vortex in Sedona that's swirling a little bit faster because I believe.

Extending my left arm over the map, I let the pendulum dangle straight down. Next, I form the question in my mind, careful to be very specific. *Where is the woman who was once known as Heidi Faulk and lived in Riparian Knolls?*

The pendulum begins to spin in a counterclockwise motion.

Erick inhales sharply, but manages to keep silent.

The swinging continues in a larger and larger circle, pulling my hand toward the northeast corner. I allow my hand to move, but the circles do not grow smaller. The pendulum doesn't snap to a point on the map, as I've seen it do in the past. The circles continue and my hand eventually reaches the edge of the map.

I exhale with exasperation. "All right, not in the Phoenix Metro area. Let's try Maricopa County." I set the pendulum down, push the city map to the side, and open up the larger, county map.

To Erick's credit, he remains as quiet as a church mouse.

I smooth the map, take my cleansing breaths, extend my arm over the new geography, and let the pendulum drop. I pose the same question, because I'm sure it has all the necessary elements for clarity.

The pendulum begins to swing more slowly and in smaller circles. My hand feels an invisible thread drawing it toward the Northeast. As I reach the corner of Maricopa County, the circles tighten and the hairs on the back of my neck ripple with energy. The circles become an arc, and the arc shrinks to a smaller and smaller measure, until, at last, the tip of the pendulum snaps to a point on the map as though drawn by a magnet.

Erick murmurs under his breath.

I look down, and the tip of the pendulum is directly in the middle of a small green square labeled Mesquite Gardens Cemetery. The pendulum has delivered its message.

"Where is it?" Erick slowly rises from the floor but doesn't approach me.

"Mesquite Gardens Cemetery."

"That's not a good sign. But if she's dead, why is everyone pretending she's still alive and possibly in Australia?"

I shrug. "A giant conspiracy? An entire neighborhood involved in bumping off one woman?"

"Come on, Moon. You know how impossible it is to keep secrets in a tight-knit community. If there were even five people that knew she was dead, it would've leaked out by now."

"I mean, I'm not guaranteeing my work, Sheriff. But if you're asking me for my hunch, Mesquite Gardens is it. You want to check it out or not?"

He grabs the keys off the bedside table. "Let's check it out."

I place the pendulum back in my rucksack and throw in the map for good measure. "Give me a second to change. I don't plan on poking around a graveyard in heels."

He waits patiently, and I change in a flash. "All right. Let's go." Unfortunately, I have to leave the wig on. Once you don a wig you can't ditch it, at least not without a good shampoo and blow out.

By the time we reach Mesquite Gardens, the caretaker has departed and the gates are locked.

Not only do I get to visit a cemetery, but I also get to break into it after dark! Hooray for me.

Tossing my rucksack over, I insert a foot into the hand-stirrup that Erick supplies and he boosts me up and over the wall. I land with a not entirely painless thud on my well-padded backside.

He follows and lands next to me with the grace and power of a jungle cat.

"Show off."

"Where should we start?"

I happen to know that a pendulum doesn't work like a divining rod, but the only way I'll be able to use my extrasensory perceptions to guide us to this woman's grave is to pretend that it does. "I'll try the pendulum again. It could help, but no guarantees."

He shrugs. "You're in charge, Moon."

Removing the pendulum from the rucksack, I dangle it with my left hand, take a deep breath, and ask the source of wherever my psychic powers come from to help me find the grave of the woman who was once known as Heidi Faulk.

A tightness grips my chest, and I can feel a cord pulling from my sternum toward something unseen. Holding the decoy pendulum out in front of me, I walk toward the source of the energy attached to my torso.

We walk for several minutes and I can feel the pull increasing.

"I don't see anything, Moon. Maybe the thing's not working. We should head to the motel and come back during the day."

"Shhhh," I hiss. I can't afford any distractions right now. Erick's skepticism will have to wait. I continue dangling the pendulum and moving toward the pulsing source of the message.

We're walking next to a small row of mausoleums that run along the back of the cemetery when a fingernail moon peeks out from behind the clouds. The eerie moonlight reflects off headstones and statuary.

Suddenly, it feels as though the eyes of the dead are watching.

My focus falters and I drop the pendulum somewhere in the darkness.

Erick doesn't seem to notice.

In a half-hearted charade, I hold out my arm and force myself to focus. The pull resumes. I turn right and walk past the first two rows, turn left, and scream.

He pushes me behind him and pulls his gun before I have a chance to explain. "What is it? Who's there? Show yourself."

Grabbing a fistful of Erick's shirt, I beg to differ. "That's not something you want to say in a cemetery. All right?"

He keeps his gun drawn. "What did you see? Why did you scream?"

My throat is dry and tight, and I can't find words. I point to the moonlit headstone.

Erick steps forward and shines his phone light on the letters engraved in the grey granite. "Coraline Moon? But that's your mom's name. I thought she was cremated. So who—"

"You better call Delgado. They're gonna have to exhume this body. And I've got a hunch, and it's this: that isn't my mom in that grave."

He holsters his gun and turns toward me. "You think it's Heidi Faulk?"

I nod and beg my stomach to remain calm while my snoopiness takes another tack. "There's probably a shovel or two in the caretaker's shed. Let's bust in there, grab them, and get started."

Erick wisely chooses not to speak. Instead, he pulls me into an embrace, kisses the top of my head, and gives me a minute to process.

My shoulders sag and I lean into him for support. "Thank you for not explaining to me how long it would actually take to dig down through six feet of hardened earth with a couple of shovels. I let my movie-brain get away from me for a minute. I'm gonna sit down by this headstone while you call Delgado. I should warn you, there's no way I'm leaving this cemetery until they bring up the casket."

"Understood." Erick reverently steps away from the gravesite and places the call.

I stare at the mysterious shadows cast by the moon and have to close my eyes. *Mama, I don't know exactly what happened yet, but I know it was terrible and I'm sorry I wasn't there for you. I mean, I know I was just a kid, but I'm sure there was something I could've done, some signs I might've noticed . . .* I take a break from the pain, and from beating myself up, while I slip into the distraction of making a plan.

When Delgado gets here with the disinterment order, and they bring up this casket, I'm definitely not looking inside. But it shouldn't take them long to grab some dental records and verify if the corpse, or at this point maybe it's mostly a skeleton, is Heidi Faulk. If it's Heidi, then I know Tiffany is involved. But she's not working alone. If Tiffany had been the one to slash our tires or fire a gun through the hotel door, then she would've recognized me at her house today. Maybe not . . . The wig I wore was high quality. But Erick . . . he wasn't in disguise. There has to be an accomplice. It would've been quite easy for someone at the mortuary to call Tiffany and inform her that Cora's ashes were being claimed. Then she simply sends one of her minions to slash the tires on the *one* vehicle in the parking lot. It's not rocket science.

Erick returns and crouches beside me. "Delgado is pretty new to the force, but she has a good relationship with her chief. She thinks she can get an exhumation approved in under an hour. She promised to be here when the sun comes up. I know you said you didn't want to leave, but it's surprisingly chilly in the desert after sunset, and we didn't bring supplies."

I slip my rucksack off my shoulder and open the main compartment. "Oh ye of little faith." I pull out my hoodie, two bottles of water, a pack of crisps (I call them crisps instead of chips in honor of my mother), a candy bar, and a half-eaten pack of gummy spiders.

Erick inspects the inventory. "I'm gonna let you have those questionable looking gummies. And that hoodie definitely isn't going to fit me."

The laughter eases the tension in my shoulders. "I seem to remember someone in Pin Cherry telling me that the best way to fend off hypothermia is shared body warmth."

If the heat from Erick's blushing cheeks is any indication, we should be able to survive an arctic chill.

He tucks the hoodie around my shoulders and scoots deliciously close to me.

He's leaning against the headstone and I'm leaning against him.

And then he dangles my "lost" pendulum in front of my face. "You dropped this at least fifty paces back. How do you explain being able to find this headstone in the dark, with no magic toy?"

My mouth goes dry and my heart races.

"Are you some kind of psychic?"

The cold ground sucks the warmth from my body. "What? That's crazy." My squeaky voice hardly offers a plausible counterargument.

He drops the pendulum onto my lap. "I know what I saw."

The only way out of this greased-pig of a conversation is to pull the girl card. "I'm so overwhelmed right now. Can you just hold me? We can talk about it tomorrow. All right?"

As I shove the pendulum into my pocket, his arm encircles me and he kisses the back of my head.

Before long, his body relaxes behind me, and his breathing is soft and slow.

Touching the bare skin of his palm, my eyes burn with tears. Four runes, purposefully traced, and he would forget all his psychic suspicions.

I drag my fingers across his flesh to see if he'll wake. My chest feels tight, and the air crackles around me.

What if I lose my focus? What if he wakes up in the middle of the transmutation? What if he forgets too much?

Silas warned me about playing God. If I take this memory from Erick . . . Is a killer of the mind any better than a murderer? Maybe it's time to risk trusting someone.

The clouds drift across the moon, and an owl hoots twice.

Slipping my hand in his, I let the tears trickle down my cheeks as his warmth envelops me.

He sighs and snuggles close.

I drift off to dream in—

CHAPTER 22

THE BEEPING of a backhoe startles us both awake and Erick nearly draws his gun.

"You guys slept in a cemetery?" The weak morning light halos Detective Delgado as she shakes her head. "Remind me to never question your commitment."

We struggle to our feet and I shake the sleep prickles out of my chilled left leg.

"Step over here, guys. We need to give the backhoe room to operate."

We follow Delgado down the row of graves and she updates us on preparations to process the remains.

"I tried to reach out to Butler this morning, but he's completely off the grid."

Erick and I exchange a knowing gaze.

She puts up a hand to stop us from saying what we're all thinking. "I know. I know. It doesn't look good. But I'm one of those cops that likes to wait until all the evidence is in before I pass judgment."

Erick rubs the stubble on his chin. "That's a good policy, Delgado."

A uniformed officer brings us all coffee and I feel as though I've received *The Gift of the Magi.*

We sip our coffee and Erick brings Delgado up to speed on our visit to Riparian Knolls.

"It's not the first time that this Tiffany woman has landed on the radar. I did some more digging, but nothing ever sticks." She shakes her head and chews her bottom lip.

An unnerving scraping sound brings our conversation to a halt, and all eyes turn toward the open grave.

The backhoe driver hops out and signals some men.

Cables are dropped in and, after an unsteady beginning, they slowly winch the casket toward the surface.

The discomfort and nausea in my stomach swirl like the perfect storm.

When the coffin breaks the surface and the dirt lazily rolls off, I'm forced to run for cover.

Thankfully, when I return, everyone's too busy

budging up around the coffin to take any notice of my ashen complexion.

Two uniformed officers with latex gloves and masks step forward and crack the time capsule.

When the lid creaks open and the dust clears, the young male officer runs for the single tree at the edge of the drive.

I don't feel nearly as self-conscious now.

Delgado and Erick "glove up" and step toward the casket.

Detective Delgado turns toward me. "Most likely female, based on the stilettos."

My heart flutters. My mom would never wear stilettos. No one who worked as hard as she did could spend eight hours on their feet in a pair of towering heels. I know it's not my mom.

Erick grips Delgado's shoulder and pulls her closer to the foot of the coffin.

He points.

Despite my oogy stomach, I'm drawn forward.

She waves a uniformed officer over and he aims his torch at an urn tucked in the shadows next to the corpse's fancy shoes. The detective gently rotates it toward the light and Erick is the first to react.

He steps back and puts a hand to his forehead before turning to me. "It's your mom. The urn is engraved with her name. Do you think your grand-parents paid extra for that?"

I'd prefer to spit on the ground and curse my grandparents' name for abandoning my mother, but if that really is my mom, I'd very much like to see the urn. "Can I see it? Can you take it away from the other thing in the box and let me see it?"

Delgado calls for a large evidence bag and care-fully transfers the tarnished silver urn from the foot of the coffin into the bag. She seals it, marks it, and hands it to me. "I don't know who or what you guys picked up at that mortuary, but you'll need to bring it in."

As soon as the weight of it settles into my hands, the messages hit me with the rapid fire of a Tommy gun. This is the real deal, unlike the fake they passed us at the mortuary.

Pictures of my mother tucking me in at night.

Memories of her putting on her makeup in front of the mirror and kissing my nose before she left for work.

Macaroni and cheese in front of the television.

Popsicles on the porch in the rain.

All the muscles in my stomach tense up at once as a vision I had utterly forgotten flashes back.

My mother crouched on the floor, pulling the cover off a heating vent in the wall and tucking something inside. She replaces the vent, finger-tightens the screws, kisses her two fingers and presses them against the vent.

Three days later she was dead.

My arms go limp.

Delgado grabs the evidence bag and Erick scoops me close. "What is it?"

Ignoring the tears streaming down my cheeks, I blurt, "I have to get back into our old house. I can't explain. There's evidence— Something's in there— She hid something in there."

Delgado looks at Erick and shakes her head.

My knight in perfect blue jeans rescues me once again. "I don't have time to list off all the examples, Delgado—and trust me, I was her number one skeptic—but I've learned not to ignore her hunches. If she says she needs to get back into that house, it's in the best interest of your case to make that happen."

Trust. I made the right choice about the runes.

Delgado shakes her head. "Look, Harper, you know how this works. I need a search warrant, I need probable cause . . . It could take days."

Erick nods. "How about if the three of us go over there and see if we can talk some sense into the current resident? You've got a badge, I've got a badge, and she's got a story that could break a stone statue's heart. We don't need a warrant if we get permission."

She shrugs and hands the evidence bag to another officer.

Struggling to find my voice, I ask, "Can I have the urn? Will I get my mother's ashes back?"

"Absolutely, Moon. But it's gotta be logged into evidence and processed. I'll try to get you an ETA—after we get back from this fool's errand."

I hang onto Erick like a life preserver in a perilous ocean. "Thank you," I whisper, as my tears create dark streaks on his cotton shirt.

Delgado commandeers a squad car from one of the uniforms, and Erick is kind enough to let me ride in front.

Even though my emotions are on a rollercoaster and my empty stomach is darting between hunger and nausea, I take the opportunity to poke a little fun. "How's it feel back there, Harper?"

The occupants of the front seats enjoy a hearty laugh at his expense.

"It's worse than I imagined, but not the worst I've seen."

As we turn onto the street of my childhood, Delgado parks in front of number 630 and puts on the lights.

"Why did you hit the lights? Won't that draw attention to us?"

Before she can answer, Erick hands her a compliment. "Good thinking. They'll be doubly motivated to cooperate once they know all their neighbors are peeking out their windows."

"Exactly why I grabbed a black and white."

We hop out of the car, and Delgado releases Erick from the back seat. She approaches first and knocks firmly on the door.

A woman in her mid-thirties, with her hair in a messy bun and a crying toddler on her hip, answers the door. Her expression instantly transforms from irritation to panic when she sees the rotating cherries.

Badges are flashed.

"Good morning. I'm Detective Delgado of the Phoenix Metro PD and this is Sheriff Harper, here on special assignment. We'd like your permission to search the premises."

The flashes of red and blue catch the attention of the screaming child and his wails turn to whimpers. The woman switches him to the opposite hip and pushes the hair back from her sweaty brow. "You don't have a warrant?"

Erick takes his at-bat. "No, miss. We're investigating a murder—"

The woman steps back in shock, and tightens her grip on the child.

"It's a cold case, miss. A murder that happened over ten years ago. This woman behind me is the daughter of the victim." He gestures to me and I offer a wan smile. "They used to live in this house, and she feels quite certain that her mother may have left some helpful evidence."

Her eyes soften.

He presses his advantage and gives her a proper Midwestern smile and nod. "We're awfully pressed for time, and we'd be so grateful if you'd give us permission to look around. I promise we'll be respectful. To be clear, this in no way involves you. We need to see if we can find something that will help us bring her mother's killer to justice."

The young woman squeezes her child close and I sense a flood of motherly affection. That tangible bond between mother and child. Erick said the exact right thing.

She steps back. "Of course, come in. But please don't break anything. He puts everything in his mouth. If you leave something on the floor—"

Erick places a calming hand on her shoulder. "Like I said, miss, we'll be extremely careful."

As I step across the threshold, into the home I once shared with my mother, a wall of emotion hits me. The flashback is so powerful, I lose track of the present. Stumbling like a zombie, I turn down the hallway toward the bedroom.

Voices are saying things behind me, but the words can't reach me. I'm on the other side now. If there is a veil between worlds, I've somehow passed through. The wall-to-wall carpet in the hallway vanishes and is replaced by cheap linoleum and the blue-green carpet runner that my mom purchased at a garage sale.

I open the bedroom door.

There's my mom's bed, perfectly made as always, and there's my tinier-than-a-twin bed in the corner. A complete disaster, as always. The vision pulls me toward the vent. Reaching down I try the screws, but layers of paint and time have locked them in place.

A shadowy cloud washes over me and I feel such disappointment.

From somewhere outside this dream world, a hand reaches down. I grip the offered screwdriver as though it were a pitcher of water in a desert.

Getting straight to work on the screws, I eventually remove all four. Using the blade of the flathead, I pry the vent cover from the wall.

Dust bunnies and unmentionable insect carcasses give me pause, but once again the past erases the present and I reached into the hole that I pray is a portal to my mother.

My hand pushes through the accumulation of years.

Nothing.

I fear I've made a terrible mistake and begin to withdraw my hand—my finger brushes against something round in the corner to the left of the vent. There is a cylindrical object pressed up against the backside of the wall.

I grip, pull, and press it to my heart.

It's a tube of lipstick.

Cinnamon mocha. The color she always wore.

Erick scoops an arm around me and pulls me to my feet.

The past evaporates.

Delgado retrieves the screwdriver and replaces the vent.

He escorts me out of the home while the detective offers her thanks to the cooperative woman.

The whole thing seems like a fever dream as I'm guided back to the cruiser and Erick slips into the back seat beside me.

Delgado kills the lights and drives. "I have to say, I'm pretty glad I didn't get a warrant to retrieve a tube of lipstick." Her tone is matter-of-fact. No judgment, but no sympathy.

Erick gently cups my hand. "May I?"

I grip the tube of lipstick even tighter, but as his thumb caresses my fingers I slowly loosen my grip.

He takes the cap off the tube of lipstick, tips it upside down, and I gasp as a small flash drive drops into the palm of his hand.

Delgado's eyes are sharp in the rearview mirror. "What is it, Harper?"

"It's a flash drive. You got a laptop at home?"

"10-4."

She hits the siren and lights, and races to her private residence.

The three of us rush inside. She fires up her laptop and turns off the Wi-Fi. "Let's see the drive."

A trio of faces clusters around the blue glow of the screen.

"The drive won't mount." She clicks several menus and tries re-inserting the drive. "Nothing. It's like it doesn't exist."

The phrase "touch it" pops into my head, and I reach my left hand toward the stick.

"I already tried the other USB port."

Ignoring Delgado, I pinch the drive between my thumb and forefinger.

There's a nearly inaudible hum and the drive flickers to life.

A moment later it mounts.

"Fingerprint encrypted security. Looks like you get your smarts from your mom." Erick squeezes my shoulder.

It contains two folders, one labeled: Mizithra; the other: THE TRUTH.

Delgado hovers her mouse over "THE TRUTH." "I'd like to open this one first and see what we've got, then Erick and I can step out while you have a look in the other folder. Is that okay with you?"

I stand up and take a ragged breath. "Yeah, do it."

She opens the folder and I see everything. Without waiting for her to click on any of the individual files my mood ring burns and I know we've got it. I step back and sink onto Delgado's sofa.

She and Erick methodically go through the files one by one and their excitement grows with each file. Until it stops.

Erick stands and looks at me. "It was Hackett. It was Hackett the whole time."

My heart breaks a little and anger swirls inside me. "I saved that man's life? He killed my mother and I saved that man's life?"

Delgado replies without turning away from the screen. "It's far more likely that Tiffany killed your mother, based on the evidence of money laundering, drug trafficking and fraudulent funerary services tied to her that your mother collected here. But Hackett definitely played a huge part in the cover-up. Maybe he's feeling some remorse for his part in all of it, now that he's ill. He must've been on Tiffany's payroll. We'll bring her in and threaten her with two first-degree murder charges. I'm sure the serial numbers on those silicone implants will trace back to Heidi. Of course, without the murder weapon it'll never stick, but we've got plenty more here to take her down for good. I'm hoping that the murder charges will convince her to turn on Hackett."

"What about Butler? He tried to kill Hackett the other day." As soon as the words are out of my mouth my mood ring turns to pure ice on my left hand. I looked down and see the sign at the entrance of Sunny Cactus. "Erick, do you still have those pictures on your phone?"

He grabs the phone, taps, and swipes. "Yeah. Why?"

I rush over and take the phone out of his hand. Flicking through the images of the people exiting the retirement community where we held our impromptu stakeout, I recognize her instantly.

Zooming in on the tall, fashionably dressed redhead, I point to her face. "You know I love a disguise. And that is Tiffany, in a very nice wig. Looks like she tried to clean up her last loose end."

"Send me that picture, Harper." Delgado turns to me. "We'll leave you alone and I'll get the wheels in motion to bring in Tiffany and Hackett."

The sheriff and the detective leave me in front of the laptop, staring at a folder bearing my name. A thousand possibilities tug at my heartstrings, and I don't know if I can stand it.

At long last, I find the courage and open the

folder. There are photos, probably twenty or so JPEG files. But at the bottom is an MP4.

I launch the file and, when the video opens, somehow I find the courage to press play.

My mother's beautiful face smiles back at me from the laptop screen and her posh accent speaks to my soul.

"How's my cheesy little girl?" Her dark eyes sparkle with love and her casual golden-brown updo reminds me of Kate Beckinsale.

"I'm afraid your silly mum has gotten in over her head. I wish I hadn't, but if wishes were horses, beggars would ride." The tinkling of her strained laughter pierces my heart. She's trying so hard to keep her terrible message lighthearted.

"It would've been quite lovely to live to a ripe old age and have tea and biscuits with my grand-children. But things have gone wonky, my little lamb. I know you're a very bright girl. Don't you ever forget that. It's a dreadful shame that I may not see the amazing woman you will become, but it will happen regardless." Her voice catches and she forces a smile.

"One day you will find this. I know you'll spy me hiding it, Mitzy. You're an adorably insufferable snoop. I hope it brings you peace and brings others to justice." Her jaw clenches, and I see the dangerous glint in her eye. My mama didn't go down without a fight.

"Most of all, no matter what happens, I want you to know your mum will always love you. Even if you can't see me, sweetie—" her voice catches and her composure threatens to abandon her "—I'm there, looking down on you, bursting with pride. When you feel the hairs tingle on the back of your neck, it's your mum showing you how much I still love you." Her eyes glisten with unshed tears.

"So don't waste any time being sad or having regrets. Promise me that. What is it that you always say? 'Let me fly my freak flag, Mama.' I think that's it." She fights back the welling emotions.

"Well, I hope you do. I hope you fly it proudly, my darling Mizithra. Mama loves you." She manages to stop the recording as the first tear cascades down her alabaster cheek.

The video ends and I can't be bothered to wipe the tears from my cheeks. "I love you too, Mama," I whisper.

The hairs on the back of my neck tingle to life and tears of joy overwhelm me. All this time, even before I knew about my gifts, she was there. She was always there.

As I exhale, the raw emotions and the sleep deprivation hit me like a cannonball.

I lean back in the chair and chuckle through my tears as a box of tissues wiggles its way into view.

"I wasn't eavesdropping, Moon, but I heard you crying. Are you okay?"

Launching out of the chair and into Erick's arms, I allow myself a few more pitiful sobs before I accept the offered tissues. It is an ugly cry, and I have to blow my nose several times before I regain composure.

Delgado reenters the room. "Once again, Moon, I'm really sorry for your loss. Unfortunately, I have to take the flash drive into evidence. You'll have to come down to the station for the thumbprint activation. I'll copy all the files that your mother collected on the illegal dealings at the funeral home. Then I'll see what I can do about getting the drive released to you. But it is evidence, and I can't make any promises. Do you want to make a copy of anything before we head into the station?"

I shake my head. "I can't think clearly about that right now. I'd really like to have the drive back, but I get what you're saying." I rub my hands across my face. "I need some sleep."

Erick squeezes my shoulders. "That makes two of us. Can we get this fingerprint encryption thing handled right away?"

Delgado grabs her keys off the table. "I'll take

you back to the minivan and you can follow me to the station. It shouldn't take long."

By the time they escort Erick and me to the second floor of the Phoenix Metro Police Department, Ian Butler is waiting for us. His arms are crossed over his chest and his expression is unreadable.

"You mind explaining to me how you two managed to solve the case that I've been working on for a decade in one week?"

Erick slips a protective arm around my shoulders. "She's a woman of many talents, Butler. I find it's best to take the win and not ask too many questions."

It's hard to miss his thinly veiled reference to the conversation I weaseled out of in the graveyard last night.

Stepping forward, I extend my hand toward the senior detective.

Butler steps forward, clasps my hand and offers sincere condolences. "I'm truly sorry about what happened to your mother."

As his hand slips into mine, the memory of her funeral grips me. "You were there." I stare at the face and see the younger man from my flashback. "The cop at my mom's funeral. You were looking for something in the casket."

Butler jerks his hand from mine and steps back.

"You remember?"

"Not really the point, Butler. What were you doing?"

He wipes a hand across his brow and sighs. "Man, seems like yesterday. I had noticed some discrepancies in Hackett's reports. I'd also started to suspect that evidence was going missing. I secretly met with Cora to double check what she knew. The things she told me didn't check out with the reports Hackett was filing. She referenced a number of meetings and documents that I'd never seen." He gestures to the thumb drive in Delgado's hand. "She was supposed to bring me one of those the night she died. As you can imagine, no such device was found on the body. I went to the funeral and searched the casket in case they were trying to bury the evidence with her. Based on what she'd told me, I knew they'd been sneaking heroin into the country in the false bottoms of caskets . . . so there was some logic to my madness."

I cross my arms and eye him suspiciously. "Copy that. But if you knew about the drug operation and the fraudulent cremations and burials, and Hackett's involvement, why didn't you make an arrest?"

Before he can answer Erick supplies the reason. "Evidence, Moon. Accusations are meaningless without evidence."

Butler nods. "Especially when you're accusing a cop with twenty-five years on the force."

Delgado holds out the fingerprint-encrypted thumb drive. "Let's get this handled."

I wave her off. "All right, but what were you doing posing as his son?"

Butler rolls his head from side to side. "That's a little more complicated. When the Alzheimer's set in, I wasn't entirely convinced it was real. Checking on him at home, as a former partner on the force, was no problem. His home-care nurse was very co-operative. Once he was transferred to the facility, I knew Tiffany would be watching him and I was still searching for the missing evidence. Posing as his son was just easier. Less questions to answer. And if anyone mentioned to Tiffany that he had visitors, a son was far less suspicious than a cop."

"Understood. One more question."

Butler glances at Erick and raises an eyebrow. "You got your hands full with this one, Sheriff."

Erick laughs. "You're not wrong, but I wouldn't have it any other way."

My heart buzzes with the warmth of his admiration. "Last question, Butler, I promise. Why didn't you stop Tiffany's attempted murder at the assisted living facility? You came out right after her. You must've known."

"You'd think. But much like the story of my

other failures in this investigation, I was in the wrong place at the right time. I'd just finished visiting Hackett and was discussing a room transfer with the director, in an attempt to facilitate searching through his belongings—again. And when I finished that meeting, I left. I knew nothing about the attempt on his life until they called his 'son' later that day." He tilts his head and narrows his gaze in my direction. "I'd like to ask you how you knew about it? According to the desk nurse, you and the sheriff rushed into the facility already in emergency response mode."

Looks like it's time to dodge, duck, and dive. "Delgado, you need me to activate that drive, right?"

She nods and gestures for me to follow. As we walk toward her office, Erick and Ian share more details of the case. Once Delgado finishes transferring all the information to a secure drive, to be submitted into evidence, she throws a backup copy on her local hard drive. "That's it. We got everything. Thanks, Moon."

Following her back to the common area, I sidle up next to Erick and urge him to wrap things up.

Delgado hands the thumb drive to Butler, and a pained expression washes over his features. He steps forward and extends the drive toward me.

As I reach to take it, he leans toward me and

whispers, "We've got the information we need. So much evidence went missing during this investigation, I don't think anyone's gonna miss a decade-old drive. Do you?"

I close my hand around the drive and slip it into my pocket. "I'm not sure I know what drive you're talking about, Detective."

He steps back, and for the first time since meeting him, a broad smile spreads across his face. "Not to sound like a Wild West sheriff, but how soon are you two planning on heading out of my town?"

Erick reaches out and shakes Butler's hand appreciatively. "We're headed up to Sedona for a day or two and then we'll be out of your hair. Pin Cherry can't survive too long without the both of us."

Butler shakes his head. "Better them than us."

Delgado pops a salute at Erick. "Safe travels, Sarge."

The 'battle buddy' callback brings a smile to my face.

Erick returns the salute and tips his head in that way that insinuates tapping the brim of a hat.

It's officially time for Butch and Sundance to get out of Dodge!

CHAPTER 23

THE TWO-HOUR DRIVE NORTH, to my old stomping grounds in Sedona, gives Erick and me the perfect opportunity to debrief.

"I can't believe Butler ended up on the right side of this. Do you think he was undercover when he signed my mother's cremation order?"

Erick chews the inside of his cheek and tips his head back and forth. "That's not exactly what happened. When you and Delgado stepped away, he confirmed that Internal Affairs had launched an investigation into Hackett. They sent in Butler to play the greenhorn partner. He claims he knew nothing about a cremation and assumed Cora was buried beneath the headstone bearing her name. I don't think we'll ever know the whole truth."

"What do you think will happen to Keith Hackett?"

The muscles in Erick's jaw tighten and release twice before he replies. "I don't much care. It's bad enough that he was a dirty cop, but Tiffany's statement directly implicates him in Heidi's murder and clearly puts him at the center of covering up your mother's."

"I agree with everything you said. But there's a part of me that still feels sorry for him. The Alzheimer's has really taken a toll. The few times I caught a glimpse of him, trapped behind that disease . . . I don't know. I suppose I should hate him for taking my mom away from me, but it doesn't feel that cut and dried."

Erick's shoulders relax and he nods in half agreement. "You're a better person than me, Moon. I gotta say, I have no sympathy for Hackett. He took advantage of his position. He manipulated civilians. He made a profit in the drug trade, directly from the misery of others. Who knows how many lives or families he destroyed, turning a blind eye to the distribution of heroin and methamphetamines all over the Phoenix Metro area?"

"You're not wrong." I can't bring myself to imagine all that suffering. "What about Tiffany? Do you think she'll serve any real time?"

Erick sighs. "I'd love to say yes. It would make a fascinating science experiment to watch that evil woman age inside a jail cell without the benefit of Botox for a decade or three."

His reference to the lack of cosmetic injectables in prison definitely makes me laugh. "Within the first six months of her sentence, I picture her slowly morphing from a fifty-year-old woman who looks thirty, to a fifty-year-old woman who looks eighty! Something like the puddles of wax melting down a candle."

He laughs. "No more than she deserves."

"What do you think all those *Housewives of Scottsdale* are going to do to keep up with their manic schedules now that Tiffany's no longer supplying them with meth?"

Erick grinds his teeth and shakes his head. "Sadly, I've seen too many addicts in my day. The truth of the matter is, they'll find a new supplier by next week."

Folding my hands in my lap, I stare out the window and study the increasing elevation. When we reach the top of the grade above Black Canyon a piece of trivia pops into my head. "Hey, that's the last saguaro cactus you'll see. It's an indicator species of the Sonoran Desert, and we're climbing into the grassland and chaparral."

Erick grips the steering wheel with both hands and braces himself against a deep belly laugh. "Maybe I'm sleep deprived, but for a minute there I felt like you were channeling *Encyclopedia Brown!*"

"Whatever. Why don't you tell me everything you know about the desert?"

He reaches across the center console and squeezes my left hand. "I don't know anything about the desert. I want you to tell me every single thing that pops into your head. I might laugh, but I promise you I'll enjoy every second that I get to learn a little bit more about you."

Warm tingles start where his fingers grip my hand and travel up my arm. My heart swells with his admiration. "All right. Saddle up, cowboy."

He squeezes my hand one more time before he places both hands back on the steering wheel at the "ten and two" positions. "I thought it was real classy of Butler to slip you the thumb drive after Delgado downloaded all the documents."

My right hand presses against the lump in the pocket of my jeans. The last thing my mother left me. A special message recorded only for me. The pain in my chest will probably never go away, but the loving words on this thumb drive will make it hurt a little bit less every day. "Yeah, he really did me a solid."

Erick exhales. "First things first. Where and

what are we eating when we get to Sedona?"

A plethora of answers fight for attention inside my head. This is the first time I've been to the glorious city of red rocks as an heiress. I don't have to scrape my pennies together to buy day-old doughnuts or scrounge french fries from a friend's plate at the bar and grill. "I'm not sure how to answer that. I'm happy to show you some of the slightly lowlife places I used to hang out, but I feel a little bit like I'm coming back to my high school reunion, but in a helicopter, *Romy and Michele* style."

Surprisingly, Erick's laughter indicates he's seen the movie. "So you want to stay at a fancy hotel and eat at five-star restaurants?"

"Is that bad? Does that make me sound like a bad person?"

He shrugs. "I'm happy to be your wing man while you roll deep, but I can't keep up that pace on a public servant's salary."

"I'd like to propose a deal, Sheriff Harper. You promise to wear the tightest T-shirts you own, while we're in Sedona, and I promise to pay for everything."

He shakes his head. "Are you trying to bribe me into being arm candy?"

I raise an eyebrow and shrug one shoulder. "Technically, you're not on the job, so I don't think it's a bribe. Plus, there are worse ways to go through life."

He shakes his head. "Are you sure there's not something else I can do?" He hangs his head and his cheeks flush with embarrassment. "If it's important to you, I'll do it."

"It feels important right now. So let's call that a tentative agreement, and reserve the right to amend it as needed."

"Deal." We hook pinky fingers and shake.

As we climb in elevation and draw near our destination in red rock country, the temperature drops and the view improves dramatically.

Where Phoenix has more the appearance of a painting by one of the old Dutch Masters, one-third land and two-thirds sky, Sedona is the opposite. The striking red rock formations consume the horizon, but the azure sky, festooned with white cotton-candy clouds, holds its own magic.

Erick lets out a low whistle. "You lived here? Why would you ever leave?"

"Spoken like a true tourist, Sheriff. One thing you'll learn about Sedona: it's a lot like an aging Hollywood actress. The first impression is striking, but the deeper you dig the more you uncover the dark secrets and nasty skeletons nobody wants to let out of the closet. Not to mention the economic disparity and the unusually high percentage of weirdos."

"Weirdos? Like what?"

"Let me break it down for you in a segment I like to call, 'Only in Sedona.'"

He chuckles. "Please, continue."

"Only in Sedona will you see a man eating lunch in a full wizard costume, complete with pointed hat."

Erick's eyes widen.

I nod and gesture in a simmer-down motion. "Only in Sedona will you walk into a grocery store and simultaneously see a six-foot-tall shirtless man, in teeny tiny hot pink shorty shorts AND a woman with daisies braided into her hair, smelling of patchouli."

Erick shakes his head and nods for me to continue.

"Only in Sedona can you peek under the tunic of a bronze sculpture of a shaman and discover he's anatomically correct. I could go on, but it's probably best that you experience it for yourself."

His laughter continues as we approach the first of many roundabouts.

"I look forward to it. Is this Sedona? Are we stopping?"

"This is the Village of Oak Creek. I brought you

this way so you could see all of the rock formations as we drive into Sedona proper."

"And what do locals call Sedona?"

"Good question. They refer to it as Slow-dona. The area has more than its share of retirees, and they pretty much roll up the streets by 8:00 p.m. There are pockets of nightlife, but it's an area known for its beauty, not its club scene."

We share a laugh, and I call out the names of the rock formations as we drive by. "Courthouse Butte, Bell Rock, Cathedral Rock, Ship Rock . . . I'm sure you see a theme developing."

Erick's stomach growls and he shoots me a guilty look. "What's the ETA on picking a place to eat?"

"Turn right into this place and we'll grab some Mexican food. I have to stock up while I'm here. What passes for Mexican cuisine in almost-Canada is barely a shadow of the real thing. We'll have some prickly-pear margaritas and *cochinita pibil* made with *javelina*, and then I'll show you where I used to work."

He parks the car and leans across the center console to whisper, "Do I want to know what a '*javelina*' is?"

"Not before you eat it." I laugh and wink. "But if we don't see one, alive, by the end of the day, I'll allow you to search the internet for images."

He chuckles and we exit the vehicle.

The meal is fantastic, and I'm enjoying sharing my Sedona secrets with Erick.

After lunch we drive to the Hot Kafka for a cup of coffee.

Walking toward the door Erick grabs my hand and pulls me to stop. "This place is called Crow's Coffee. Did we make a wrong turn?"

Subconsciously I had noticed, but the name doesn't matter. "Oh, right. I should've mentioned, businesses open and close faster than the doors on a cuckoo clock in this town. Apparently there's not a great deal of 'running of the numbers' prior to the launching of businesses. So I'm mildly surprised that Hot Kafka is gone, but it lasted longer than its predecessors."

Erick looks from the new sign to me. "So it was other stuff before your coffee shop?"

"Technically, it wasn't my coffee shop. I just worked there. And I was a pretty crappy employee, to be honest. But yes it was many things. And I can only tell you what I know from my short stint in this town. Who knows what it was before I arrived? When I first moved here it was a Greek restaurant called 'You're My Gyro.' They folded and were replaced by a beverage purveyor, 'Colossal Teas.' Possibly the most pretentious group of people I'd ever met, which is certainly why they barely lasted three months. Then I think it was another coffee shop called 'I O U a Cuppa Joe,' but they actually folded before they opened, if memory serves. And then it was Hot Kafka. It's kind of a shame it's already closed. I would've super loved for you to meet my SUPER-visor Dean. He was a real trip."

We step into the coffee shop and walk to the counter to order our beverages. Imagine my surprise when our barista turns out to be none other than the aforementioned Dean. This is what is known as a true "Sedona Moment."

"Welcome to Crow's Coffee. Where are you visiting us from today?"

A smug grin creeps across my face. "Hey, Dean. We'll take two coffees, black, with room for cream in mine."

The satisfaction of watching his little mouth open and close like a fish struggling to breathe out of water is indescribable.

Erick leans down to make eye contact with Dean and blasts him with a thousand watts of Midwestern charm. "How about we make those raven-size, whatever that is."

Dean's pale, thin lips eventually stop flapping and he somehow manages to type in the order and squeak out a total.

Erick is ready with a crisp twenty, while I cross my arms and continue to grin like the Joker.

Dean passes Erick the change, and my wonderful boyfriend shoves all of it in the tip jar.

I want to turn and hug him until he can't breathe. That's exactly what I was hoping he would do. I strut over to a shiny new bistro table and take a seat, while Erick grabs a couple of napkins before joining me.

When he sits down, I put a hand up to screen my mouth from the counter and whisper across the table. "That was amazing."

He nods toward our barista. "Is that *the* Dean?"

I nod and giggle.

He leans toward me and his blue-grey eyes sparkle with mischief. "I feel like there's a story here you're not telling me."

My giggling stops and I bite my lower lip as images of my last day of employment at the Hot Kafka flash in a shocking montage.

Late.

Stained uniform.

Punishment dished out by Dean.

Newly minted heiress realizes she doesn't need her minimum wage job.

Uniform shirts may or may not have been angrily removed and tossed.

Resignations were definitely made.

Not my finest hour. Not sharing that story with Sheriff Too-Hot-To-Handle.

"He was an over-zealous manager, all right. We called him SUPER-visor Dean because he's always saying everything was so 'super.' I didn't leave on the best of terms."

Erick nods knowingly. "I can imagine."

My cheeks redden. "Please don't."

Dean approaches the table and tentatively sets down our two enormous mugs of coffee. "Mitzy? It is you, isn't it?"

I glance toward him and nod real slowly. "It is."

"Well, gosh, it sure is super great to see you again. I hung on to your last paycheck from Hot Kafka for three months. But then they expire and it was super hard to find you. No forwarding address, you know. I sure hope everything turned out okay."

"That was super nice of you, Dean. Everything turned out great. Namaste."

Dean immediately places his hands together in prayer pose and performs a shallow bow—"Namaste"—before he wanders away.

Erick's face is a mix of shock and suppressed glee. "You were being facetious, right?"

"Entirely." I pour the cream in my coffee and watch it swirl through the rich black depths.

He exhales. "That's a relief. For a minute there, I thought I lost you."

We finish our surprisingly acceptable coffee

and hit a few more tourist hotspots as I show him around.

About 3:00 in the afternoon, the bright skies shift to darkness and a massive roll of thunder sends chills down my spine. A crack of lightning splits open the sky and rain dumps from the heavens.

We rush under an overhang in front of one of the area's many art galleries and I grip Erick's hand as I close my eyes.

"This is the best part of Sedona."

He slips an arm around my waist and pulls me close.

As the monsoon rages, the temperature drops and little goosebumps pop up on my skin.

"We should get you back in the van. I can turn the heat on."

The film-school dropout in me screams for vindication. I step out into the flower-ringed courtyard and let the water flood over me.

Erick joins me and pulls me close.

I tilt up my head.

His lips meet mine . . .

And, scene. Cut. Print. That's a wrap.

He's ready to call it a day and head back to our hotel, but I promise him that the desert winds will clear out the clouds, and we'll be enjoying a gorgeous Southwest sunset before he can name five types of cactus.

After a warm up in the van, we order take out from a local burger joint and grab some hard ciders at the grocery store.

The rainclouds have passed, and the fresh smell of the wet creosote bushes fills the air. I'm so glad I saved my secret sunset spot for the end of our perfect day.

With the hatch open, we sit in the back of our white minivan, drinking hard cider and watching the sky shift from brightest blue, to golden orange, to fiery pink, before slipping to sweetest indigo.

Tomorrow we'll board an airplane and return to Pin Cherry Harbor. I'll go back to owning a bookshop, living with a nosy ghost, and using my psychic abilities to solve crimes whenever I can. Erick will return to being the sheriff of Birch County, and I'm not entirely sure what that means for our relationship.

I'm certain Grams will have plenty of suggestions.

My hand slides into the pocket of my jeans and I rub the small thumb drive as though it's some type of magical talisman.

Now that I have a part of my mother, her last words to me, it feels as though I can put a piece of my past to rest.

I don't know what the future holds, but right

now all my senses can confirm that a whole new adventure is beginning.

And, I'm all in!

End of Book 9

But, the mysteries continue...
Curl up with the next book in the Mitzy Moon
Mysteries series!

A NOTE FROM TRIXIE

Yeehaw! Another case solved! I'll keep writing them if you keep reading . . .

The best part of "living" in Pin Cherry Harbor continues to be feedback from my early readers. Thank you to my alpha readers/cheerleaders, Angel and Michael. HUGE thanks to my fantastic beta readers who continue to give me extremely useful and honest feedback: Veronica McIntyre, Renee Arthur, and Nadine Peterse-Vrijhof. And big "small town" hugs to the world's best ARC Team – Trixie's Mystery ARC Detectives!

Heaps of down-home gratitude to my editor, Philip Newey. I always look forward to Philip's straightforward, no-nonsense feedback. Another THANK YOU to Brooke for her tireless proofreading! Any errors are my own.

You can all thank the infuriating javelina that invade and destroy my beautiful garden for the *cochinita pibil*!

I'm currently writing book eleven in the Mitzy Moon Mysteries series, and I think I may just live in Pin Cherry Harbor forever. Mitzy, Grams, and Pyewacket got into plenty of trouble in book one, *Fries and Alibis*. But I'd have to say that book three, *Wings and Broken Things*, is when most readers say the series becomes unputdownable.

I hope you'll continue to hang out with us.

Trixie Silvertale (September 2020)

LIES AND PUMPKIN PIES

Mitzy Moon Mysteries #10

When a broomball rivalry turns deadly, can this psychic sleuth save the man she loves?

Mitzy Moon doesn't do sports, but girlfriends are supposed to try new things. And watching her handsome sheriff's team strut their stuff across the ice has its perks. But the thrill fades faster than cheap lipstick when the opponent's captain is found murdered, and her boyfriend is the prime suspect.

With no alibi, her main squeeze quickly loses his badge and gets tossed off the case—and the harder Mitzy digs for the truth, the guiltier he looks. She'll need the help of her interfering Ghost-ma and a spoiled feline to clear her beau and still have time to make a special pie for the holiday potluck!

Can Mitzy score a win for the home team, or will her dreams of a clean sweep be forever frozen?

Lies and Pumpkin Pies is the tenth book in the hilarious paranormal cozy mystery series, Mitzy Moon Mysteries. If you like snarky heroines, supernatural intrigue, and a dash of romance, then you'll love Trixie Silvertale's twisty whodunit.

Buy *Lies and Pumpkin Pies* to serve up a Thanksgiving caper today!

Grab yours here!
readerlinks.com/l/5212004

Scan this QR Code with the camera on your phone. You'll be taken right to the next case!

Once you're in the Club, you'll also be the first to receive updates from Pin Cherry Harbor and access to giveaways, new release announcements, behind-the-scenes secrets, and much more!

Scan this QR Code with the camera on your phone. You'll be taken right to the page to join the Club!

THANK YOU!

Trying out a new book is always a risk and I'm thankful that you rolled the dice with Mitzy Moon. If you loved the book, the sweetest thing you can do (*even sweeter than pin cherry pie à la mode*) is to leave a review so that other readers will take a chance on Mitzy and the gang.

Don't feel you have to write a book report. A brief comment like, "Can't wait to read the next book in this series!" will help potential readers make their choice.

★★★★★
Leave a quick review HERE
https://readerlinks.com/l/1313027
★★★★★

Thank you kindly, and I'll see you in Pin Cherry Harbor!

Mitzy Moon Mysteries

Paranormal Cozy Mysteries

Fries and Alibis

Tattoos and Clues

Wings and Broken Things

Sparks and Landmarks

Charms and Firearms

Bars and Boxcars

Swords and Fallen Lords

Wakes and High Stakes

Tracks and Flashbacks

Lies and Pumpkin Pies

Hopes and Slippery Slopes

Hearts and Dark Arts

Dames and Deadly Games

Castaways and Longer Days

Schemes and Bad Dreams

Carols and Yule Perils

Dangers and Empty Mangers

Heists and Poltergeists

Blades and Bridesmaids

Scones and Tombstones

Vandals and Yule Scandals

Harper and Moon Investigations
Paranormal Cozy Mysteries

Ropes and Last Hopes

Bells and Bombshells

Rodeo Clowns and Shakedowns

Stiffs and Petroglyphs

Fatal Wines and Valentines

April Curses and May Hearses

Wheels and Dirty Deals

Scripts and Empty Crypts

Christmas Catastrophe Mysteries
Culinary Cozy Mysteries

Peppermint Cookie Murder

Apple Dumpling Murder

Linzer Cookie Murder

Chocolate Crinkle Cookie Murder

...more to come!

MAGICAL RENAISSANCE FAIRE MYSTERIES

Explore the world of Coriander the Conjurer. A fortune-telling fairy with a heart of gold!

Book 1:

All Swell That Ends Spell – A dubious festival. A fatal swim. Can this fortune-telling fairy herald the true killer?

Book 2:

Fairy Wives of Windsor – A jolly Faire. A shocking murder. Can this furtive fairy outsmart the killer?

Book 3:

Double Double Royal Trouble – When a treat-peddling witch is found dead, will this cursed faire crumble?

Join Sydney Coleman and her unruly ghosts, as they solve mysteries in a truly haunted mansion!

Book 1: ***Moonlight and Mischief*** – She's desperate for a fresh start, but is a mansion on sale too good to be true?

Book 2: ***Moonlight and Magic*** – A haunted Halloween tour seem like the perfect plan, until there's murder...

Book 3: ***Moonlight and Mayhem*** – An unwelcome visitor. A surprising past. Will her fire sale end in smoke?

ABOUT THE AUTHOR

USA TODAY Bestselling author Trixie Silvertale grew up reading an endless supply of Lilian Jackson Braun, Hardy Boys, and Nancy Drew novels. She loves the amateur sleuths in cozy mysteries and obsesses about all things paranormal. Those two passions unite in all her cozy mysteries, and she's thrilled to write them and share them with you.

When she's not consumed by writing, she bakes to fuel her creative engine and pulls weeds in her herb garden to clear her head (*and sometimes she pulls out her hair, but mostly weeds*).

Greetings are welcome:
trixie@trixiesilvertale.com

f facebook.com/TrixieSilvertale

o instagram.com/trixiesilvertale

BB bookbub.com/authors/trixie-silvertale

www.ingramcontent.com/pod-product-compliance
Lightning Source LLC
Chambersburg PA
CBHW021947170626
46808CB00001B/51